SIREN
Publishing

Marla

Ménage Everlasting

CAUGHT BETWEEN HAWK and GUNNER

2

The Howling Death MC

Caught Between Hawk and Gunner

Jackie's looking for a new start. Hawk and Gunner weren't looking for anything, but they sure as hell found her. Can they keep her?

Jackie's life hasn't been smooth, but she's determined to find a new one with fewer bumps in the road. When her truck breaks down and she accepts a ride from two bikers, all of her plans are upended in a little dusty town in the middle of nowhere.

Hawk likes what he sees, but his partner Gunner is resistant for some reason. When danger is knocking at their back gate, the two men are tasked with keeping a close eye on Jackie. Could she be a spy for their enemy, or is she just an innocent bystander with enough baggage to kill a horse?

The three have to work it all out before their fighting leads to someone falling into the wrong hands. Hawk and Gunner aren't letting Jackie go. Now, they just have to convince her.

Genre: Contemporary, Ménage a Trois/Quatre
Length: 45,470 words

CAUGHT BETWEEN HAWK AND GUNNER

The Howling Death MC 2

Marla Monroe

Siren Publishing, Inc.
www.SirenPublishing.com

ABOUT THE AUTHOR

Marla Monroe has been writing professionally for nearly thirteen years. Her first book with Siren was published in January 2011, and she now has over 75 books available with them. She loves to write and spends every spare minute either at the keyboard or reading. She writes everything from sizzling-hot cowboys, emotionally charged BDSM, and dangerously addictive shifters to science fiction ménages with the occasional badass biker thrown in for good measure.

Marla lives in the southern US and works full-time at a busy hospital. When not writing, she loves to travel, spend time with her feline muses, and read. Although she misses her cross-stitch and putting together puzzles, she is much happier writing fantasy worlds where she can make everyone's dreams come true. She's always eager to try something new and thoroughly enjoys the research she does for her books. She loves to hear from readers about what they are looking for in their reading adventures.

E-mail:
themarlamonroe@yahoo.com

Website:
www.marlamonroe.com

Blog:
www.themarlamonroe.blogspot.com

Twitter:
@MarlaMonroe1

Facebook:
www.facebook.com/marla.monroe.7

CAUGHT BETWEEN HAWK AND GUNNER

The Howling Death MC 2

MARLA MONROE
Copyright © 2017

Chapter One

"Where the hell is a cop when you need one?" Jackie Culpepper stared at the spewing radiator of her old Ford truck in disgust.

Jackie, Jack to everyone who knew her back in Roeho, Texas, sighed and looked toward the heavens, blowing the wild, unmanageable hair out of her eyes as she did. How had her perfect life gone so wrong? She snorted.

As if. I can't remember a day that I haven't had to fix, fight, or fuss about something. Damn, I can't remember the last time I closed my eyes and relaxed for longer than five freaking minutes.

Looking back down at the rust bucket of a truck, Jackie wished she'd had enough money to do a complete overhaul on the thing, but the green stuff sure as shit didn't grow on trees. She'd fixed everything she could afford to like changing the spark plugs, air filter, fuel filter, and getting brand new tires. Leave it to her stellar luck to have the one thing she didn't think would be a problem to blow a hole and wag its tongue at her.

She stared down the road where she'd come from but didn't see a single hint that someone might be heading her way. Turning toward the direction she'd been heading, the view looked the same, miles and miles of empty road with nothing between her and the next town other than flat land and a crap load full of empty promises.

Oh and don't forget that freaking hot sun. I can't believe I'm going to end up walking. How many more miles is it to the next god forsaken spit puddle on the map?

Jackie stomped around to the cab of the truck and leaned in to pull out the taped together printouts she'd made at the library. Maps were expensive. Looking at where she'd last been and where she thought she was now, it looked to be another six to eight miles to some Podunk town called Settler's Point, Oklahoma.

"Just great. I can't carry all of my shit that far." She squeezed her eyes shut for a second to make sure she wasn't about to pull a girl and cry over some stupid crap like this.

She folded the map and shoved it back into the glove compartment before pulling her pack off the passenger side seat. Jackie stuffed everything valuable into the pack that already held a change of clothes for emergencies like this. She'd weathered enough of them to keep a go-bag with her at all times.

What had she expected anyway? Her entire life had been living between one disaster after another. She'd no sooner make it through one and catch her breath before the next one was bearing down on her at warp speed. She didn't know if she could function on anything but high alert. What if quiet solitude annoyed her? What if she finally found a place to settle down without the drama of her extended family or the constant nagging from some bill collector or another? What if for once she found friends who didn't back stab her? Could she live without constant chaos?

"I sure as hell would like to find out," she grumbled.

Jackie locked the truck after taking one last look to be sure she had everything of absolute importance. She slipped on the much heavier backpack and started walking toward the next town.

The first mile wasn't so bad. Yeah, she was sweating, and her crazy hair wouldn't stay out of her face even after she'd stuck most of it under a cap, but all in all, a decent mile. The second one passed about like the first, but with a little more sweat and the pack was starting to get heavy.

By the fourth mile, Jackie was breathing hard and cursing the truck under her breath as she tried to find a dry place on her shirt to wipe the sweat out of her stinging eyes. Why in the hell had she thought she could walk eight miles?

At first she thought it was the heat making her ears ring, but once she stopped talking to herself, Jackie was sure she could hear the roar of pipes. Motorcycles. She turned to look over her shoulder, and a watery mirage of bikes appeared on the road in the distance, quickly eating up the road between them.

"Damn. There isn't anything tall enough to hide me even if they haven't already seen me. Maybe they'll ride right by. I hope." She turned and continued walking. "I'm screwed."

Jackie knew the rumble as they drew closer meant more than four or five. When the ground beneath her feet began to vibrate, she steeled herself for whatever happened next.

Maybe I'll get lucky for once in my crazy life, and they'll just grin as they drive by. I won't even shoot them the bird. All they have to do is keep on riding.

Two of the bikes passed her going slow enough they could have walked the damn things. When they turned, pulling off onto the side, stopping a good ten yards ahead of her, she knew she was in a world of crap. Two more bikes slow-motored past to stop on the edge of the road about five yards from her. The crunch of gravel behind her told her that at least one bike had pulled over behind her.

She stopped where she was but didn't turn around. Instead, she slipped one hand into her pocket and pulled out her CAT punch, a handheld weapon shaped like a cat's head where the ears were sharp points, and continued to look at the ground a couple of yards ahead of her. Deafening silence startled her when they all cut their engines at the same time. The only thing she could hear was the sound of her heart beating in her ears over the noise of her teeth grinding as she clenched them.

I'm so fucked!

The two bikers ahead of her hadn't moved. When she risked looking up, she could see that they hadn't removed their helmets either. That was good, she figured. If she couldn't identify them, maybe they wouldn't kill her. As long as she was alive, she would survive. That had been her motto nearly her entire twenty-nine years.

The two bikers who had stopped right next to her slowly pulled off their helmets. She had to roll her lips in over her teeth to keep from screaming at them to keep their helmets on. Instead, she made sure she didn't turn toward them, watching them from the corner of her eye just to be sure they didn't approach her. She had no idea what she could do if they did. There was nowhere to run even if she could outrun a bike. The CAT punch would probably only make them madder even if she managed to get one good hit in.

"That your truck back there, sweetheart?" one of the men next to her asked.

Good lord, his voice alone could cause a woman to climax. She wouldn't even need to see his face or body. That deep rumble was enough to reach right through a woman's clothes and rub her pussy to orgasm all by itself.

I'm so screwed.

"Yeah. It's mine." She had to swallow before she could even answer. Her throat felt drier than the lint screen on a clothes dryer.

"Need a ride into town?" the other biker asked. While his voice wasn't as drool-worthy as the man next to him, Jackie still ended up with chill bumps all down her back.

It took a monumental effort not to shiver at the sensation. All she needed was for them to think she was scared spitless of them. Even though she was, letting them know it wouldn't be good for her in the long run. She needed to remain calm and keep her temper in check. Pissing off a biker was stupid. Pissing off a biker with six or eight of his buddies around him was right on up there with the world's stupidest criminal's award. Oh, they called those the Darwin Awards, didn't they.

"Yeah, thanks, but I'm good. I appreciate the offer, though." Jackie cringed at how hollow her voice sounded. Even a blond could hear the fear in it.

"Look, hon. It's hot out here, and you've still got a good six or so miles ahead of you. Just climb on, and we'll drop you off wherever you want. The garage is open, but it won't be by the time you walk all the way there carrying that pack." That deep voice had her squeezing her legs together. She almost missed what he was saying.

"Um, what time is it?" She couldn't believe she'd just asked a biker what time it was. What was wrong with her? Where was her sense of self-preservation that had been working fine until a few seconds ago?

"Looks like about four. You're soaking wet, and cowboy boots aren't exactly good for walking long distances. You'll have blisters before you get there. Hop on, hon." She couldn't help looking over to see what the man with the slow, smooth voice looked like.

She'd figured the panty-soaker voice to be the one farthest from her, and the smooth talker was the one closest to her. When she finally looked up and in their direction, Jackie couldn't believe her eyes. Two of the most handsome men she'd ever seen sat straddling serious muscle.

The biker closest to her had a square jaw with a small scar diagonally across his chin. It didn't detract from his rugged good looks one iota. A scruffy shadow outlined the thin imperfection, or she wouldn't have noticed it at all. His eyes didn't waver as she took him in—all of him. Their intense, fathomless black stare would have unnerved anyone, but for some reason, it didn't scare her. She had a difficult time pulling her gaze away.

He had short brown hair that looked as if it had gray highlights and was standing up in a perfect helmet-head style. His broad shoulders tapered down to a narrow waist, and the cut of his jeans put those thick muscular thighs on display perfectly. She wished he wasn't on the bike so she could see his ass and just maybe get an idea of what his package would be like.

What. The. Fuck. Why am I ogling a biker who very well might torture and kill me? Have I already managed to get sunstroke?

"We aren't going to hurt you, sweet thing. Let us get you to town before the garage closes." Her eyes snapped to the other man as his rich voice thrummed across nerve endings she didn't even know she had.

"I—I think I'll take my chances walking. Thanks, though."

"Gunner," a deep, sinful voice said.

Before she could wonder what he was talking about, the biker closest to her threw one leg back over the seat and two strides later, he had her left wrist in his huge paw of a hand, pulling her toward his bike. Jackie nearly panicked, forgetting all about her CAT punch. Instead of stopping at his bike, the huge man pulled her around it to stand next to Mr. Fuck Me with Your Voice.

Jackie finally caught up with what was happening and pulled out the punch, aiming it for the biker's ribs. It connected, but instead of going through a T-shirt and into his side, it stopped dead, jarring her wrist so that she cried out. What the hell did he have on? Surely the leather vest wasn't made of chain mail. Fuck that had hurt!

"Son of a bitch!" her captor snarled. "What the fuck are you doing, babe? Trying to kill me?"

He wrapped his arms around her in a bear hug and yanked the CAT punch from her weakened grip, tossing it over to his partner. She looked up at the man still straddling his bike to see an amused expression.

Not good, Jackie. Not good at all.

The biker holding her slowly relaxed his grip and turned her around to face him. Although he looked pissed as hell, he didn't appear to be ready to kill her right away. He just stared down at her face as if searching for something. Then he shook his head as if he hadn't found it and sighed.

"That was stupid. You know that, right?" he asked.

Evidently he wasn't expecting her to answer because he turned her back around, jerked off her cap, and shoved the helmet on her head the other biker handed him from out of his saddle bag before patting the seat behind his friend.

"Climb on, darling. No getting out of it now."

Jackie had ridden the back of a bike enough to know how to get on and what to keep her feet and legs away from, but those had been consensual rides where she was more than happy to hang on tight to the guy doing the driving. This was riding on the back of a stranger's bike she hadn't wanted to get on in the first place, knowing she had to wrap her arms around him or risk falling off.

Weighing road rash against getting up close and personal with a man who could melt your panties off with a single word didn't really present much of a choice. Even if the man was a biker, she liked her skin intact, so without being prompted, Jackie wrapped her arms around the man and prayed they actually did stop at the garage in town.

"You good with the pack or do you want me to take it for you?" the other biker asked.

"I'm good. Thanks," she added as an afterthought.

She figured being nice and polite couldn't hurt. It might not help, but it sure as fuck couldn't hurt. Right?

As soon as the other man had gotten back on his bike, sans helmet, they started their bikes without one word and pulled back onto the road, heading in the right direction. At least one thing was going her way. She prayed it wouldn't be the last.

* * * *

Hawk couldn't believe the beauty he had sitting behind him on his bike. He hadn't really been able to see much of her with that cap pulled down over her eyes, but she had some wicked curves he'd love to get his hands and mouth on. Damn but he was hard as fuck. Watching her ass as they'd slowly ridden up on her had just about made him forget to hold on and control his bike. That sweet, squeezable butt swayed just the right amount to be natural and not a come-hither shake.

Fuck me!

The feel of her breasts pressed against his back didn't help his current condition. Even through her shirt, his shirt, and his leather cut, there was no disguising the plush softness that was currently massaging his back as they rode over bumpy asphalt. She'd ridden on the back of a bike before he surmised by the fact that she'd wrapped her arms around him despite not feeling safe with him and moved with the motion of the bike. Most women tended to grasp at his side believing they could get away with not hugging him that way. This beauty knew better and had determined he was better than skinned flesh that would mean hours of picking rocks and asphalt out of it.

"H, man. That is one fine piece of ass riding behind you. Just wait until you get a good look of her. She has more curves than a mountain road. We could ride her for hours and not see all the sights I bet she has to offer."

Hawk smiled. He was glad they were on their private frequency. The other guys wouldn't let them forget about the one who got away, 'cause Hawk already knew she wouldn't stick around.

"Keep your dick in your pants, Gunner. She won't have the time of day for a couple of kind of reformed bikers. No use giving the others a reason to rag our asses. If they find out how much she affects you, they'll piss you off in no time, and Rage and Terror will bust your ass for fighting. Simmer down, buddy." Hawk hated that the first time his friend had shown any interest in a woman after Peggy had died, it would be a drifter who was scared to death of them in the first place.

"Not going to happen, man. I can lust after her all I want with you and in my head. Don't mean I'm stupid enough to show it to the brothers," Gunner told him with a snort. "Get real, Hawk. Now tell me what she feels like all pressed up against your back like she is. I bet them tits are drool-worthy."

Hawk chuckled. "Like a wet dream. You feeling it? Her breasts are real. They're soft and large enough to really enjoy without fear they'll suffocate you when she's on top."

Gunner's strained groan echoed over the mic. "Fuck you, man. The bike is vibrating a little too good against my balls right now."

"Fuck, you've got it easy over there. My balls are vibrating just as much as yours, but I have a woman plastered to my back with her arms wrapped around me. I swear I can feel the heat from her pussy against my ass."

"You ain't right, man. You know that, don't you." Gunner growled across the radio. "What I wouldn't give to taste that pussy. I bet it's sweet as molasses."

"I don't know, G. I think she's got a little sass in her. I bet she tastes rich and spicy," he teased his friend.

"Don't say that. You know how much I like a sassy woman. You better hope she doesn't mouth off before we leave her at the garage," Gunner warned.

"Forget it, man. We don't need that kind of trouble." Hawk had been teasing. He sure as hell didn't expect his friend to get serious about the woman.

"Hey, you started it, bro," Gunner said.

Holy fuck! What was I thinking? If she so much as looks at him wrong, he's going to be all over her. Sometimes I should keep my mouth closed.

As soon as they pulled up outside the garage, his little rider jumped down off his bike so fast he hadn't even managed to cut the engine. The rest of the gang rode on past, heading to the club on the opposite end of town. He climbed off just as Gunner walked over to take the helmet from the woman's hands.

Hawk swore he didn't see it coming, but he should have, and he couldn't have stopped it if he'd wanted to.

Chapter Two

"Whoa! Stop right where you are. I appreciate the ride, but I don't like being manhandled into one." Jackie wanted to slam her hand over her mouth.

What the hell am I doing? Why on earth would I want to rile these two huge bikers up like that? Do I have a death wish or something? I've got enough to deal with without adding two pissed off reprobates to the list.

Jackie had one hand out as if she could stop a roaring train, and the other held the helmet which she extended behind her toward the other man. She just prayed he'd take it and call off the other one.

"Aw, little darling. Was I too rough on you? Let me see your hand so I can kiss the boo-boo and make it better," the scowling biker said before reaching out to grab her outstretched hand.

Jackie tried to jerk it back when she realized what he was going to do, but she wasn't fast enough. The man had lightning-fast reflexes, that was for sure. He'd snatched her hand and pulled her until she'd lost her balance so that she ended up holding on to him so she wouldn't fall. His amused chuckle didn't calm her down one bit.

She looked up at the oddly handsome face despite the scruffy look and the small scar. As he looked at her, she could see that those dark eyes were black as midnight and appeared deeper than an abyss. He had to be about six feet three with muscles on top of muscles. Everything about him from the intense stare to the leather vest with its various patches and pins screamed danger, danger. Turn back, Jackie. But she was caught, and she knew it.

"Be still," he said.

Jackie immediately turned into a statue and almost held her breath. The mountain of a man looked at the back of her hand to her wrist and farther up her arm without saying a thing. Then he slowly turned it over to check the underside, as well. She knew the instant he saw it by the way he froze and the quick intake of breath. To her surprise, he grabbed her other arm and turned it over to check that one, as well.

"What the fuck!" The biker dropped her hands and stared down at her. "Don't need that shit. Tell the guy in the garage The Howling Death MC sent you. He'll take care of you."

"My CAT punch!" she yelled.

He pulled it out of a pocket somewhere and tossed it to her before he stomped over to his bike and climbed on. He'd barely gotten his helmet on, not even securing the strap before he'd started the big bike up and was pulling out of the lot. The other biker stared at her from where he still sat as if she'd grown horns or something. She could tell he had black hair and dark eyes, but she couldn't tell much more before he, too, took off.

Jackie wasn't sure how long she stood there in the middle of the gravel lot listening to the fading sound of the two bikes, but someone cleared their throat behind her, so she turned around.

"What kin I do for you, lady?" a wrinkled old man asked with a wild twang in his voice.

"Um, my truck died on the way here about eight or so miles down the road. Radiator sprung a leak. Can you tow it in and fix the radiator for me?" she asked.

"Sure thing on towing her in, but can't be sure 'bout the radiator till I take a look see." The man turned and slowly walked bowlegged back to the garage without saying anything more. Jackie figured she was supposed to follow him, so she headed in that direction, still wondering why the bastard's reaction to her scars had affected her so much.

She was used to pity and worried looks and even sneers, but the anger that had been on the man's face puzzled her, and if she were honest, it had disappointed her a little. Why? She didn't know him and was positive she'd never see him again. They were probably passing through just like she was. So why did his reaction hurt?

"Wanna ride along or wait for me here?" the wizened old man asked her as he climbed up behind the wheel of a huge wrecker.

"Is there a motel around here?" she asked as she pulled the truck key out of her pocket.

"Sure is. Just down the street there," he said pointing in the same general direction the bikes had gone.

"Here's the key to the truck. Can't miss it. I'm going to find a room for the night. What time should I come back to check on my truck?"

"Hmm, won't look at it tonight, so better wait till close to noon so I have time to look at what I can do," he said, scratching his chin.

"Okay. Um, the guys that brought me in said to tell you The Howling Wolf MC sent me," she told him as an afterthought.

"Kinda figured that one out myself." He chuckled until he started coughing. Shaking his head, he slammed the door shut and started up the rig.

After a few jerks and a loud backfire, the wrecker pulled out of the garage and turned toward her busted truck. Jackie wasn't sure what she'd landed herself in the middle of, but just as soon as her truck was patched up and ready, she'd kick the town's dust off her boots and keep going.

The walk "just down the street there" turned into the equivalent of almost five city blocks. Normally a brisk walk didn't faze her, but after walking at least five miles in the boiling heat carrying a heavy pack on her back then riding to what she was afraid was her death on the back of a biker dude's ride, Jackie was a bit worn out. When she finally made it to the motel, she opened the door and immediately plopped down on the nearest chair.

"How much crazier can my screwed-up life get?"

She just wanted a shower, a bed, and something decent to stuff in her belly. Maybe not in that order, but as soon as possible. A noise behind her made her twist in the chair to see what it was. To her shock, a little Chinese woman watched her from behind the registration desk. Jackie figured she had to be at least a hundred years old. There were wrinkles on her wrinkles, and she wasn't sure if the tiny woman was smiling or it just looked that way due to the creases in her skin.

"You like room? How long?" the woman asked.

"Um, yes. I'm not sure. My truck broke down, so it depends on how long it takes to fix it," she told the woman.

"One night, good. You need stay more, we can do that." The woman pecked at the very old computer that took up twice as much room as a new one would have. After a few minutes, she grunted and looked up.

"How you pay?"

"Cash."

The woman held out her hand. "Need license and forty dollars."

Jackie fished out her license and two twenties then handed both to her. She pecked on the computer for another three or four minutes then handed her license back with a key that had a tennis ball attached to it by a small chain.

"Room twelve on back. Clean room, fresh sheets. I count towels so don't steal." She wagged her finger up at Jackie before turning around and disappearing through a door to one side of the desk.

"Guess that's that." Jackie was surprised there hadn't been more to the registration process than that. She didn't have to sign her name anywhere or even make up a tag number. Cash and her license.

She prayed as she walked around to the back of the motel that her room really would be clean with fresh sheets but didn't count on it. The place had to be fifty years old and could use a fresh coat of paint. She stopped in front of the door to her room and shoved the key in the lock. It turned easily, and the door didn't make a sound when she shoved it open with the toe of her boot.

Expecting stale air, Jackie had to squint to be sure she wasn't seeing things. The room looked and smelled clean and fresh. The walls weren't dingy white or puke green. Instead, a pale yellow complemented the mint green blackout curtains and bedspread.

"Just wow! Talk about not judging a book by its cover. This is nice."

She stepped all the way inside and closed the door behind her. Dropping her pack on one of the chairs next to the window, Jackie tested the queen-size bed to find it comfortable. The mattress had to be fairly new to feel that nice. Jumping up, she checked out the bathroom and wasn't disappointed. The fixtures were dated, but they were clean and it had fresh paint on the walls in there, as well. She'd really lucked up with where she'd broken down. The last place she'd stayed that hadn't been in her truck had been so bad she wasn't been able to get comfortable to sleep since she had refused to take her clothes off.

I'm going to take at least a couple of showers while I'm here just to make up for the ones I've missed.

Feeling a bit better after having seen her room, she decided to find something to eat before showering and going to bed. She was beat and hadn't managed to get much sleep the entire trip from Texas three days ago. Had it already been three days? The trip should only have taken one, but she'd taken every back road she could find and double backed on herself a couple of times before crossing into Oklahoma.

She didn't want to travel down that road again until she'd had something to eat, a nice hot shower, and clean clothes. Then she could figure out what she was going to do next. The pressures had been too much, which was why she'd left. Now she wasn't going to let them build back up because she was tired and hungry.

Grabbing her pack and the tennis ball attached to the key, Jackie locked the door behind her and strode back the way she'd come. She was pretty sure she'd seen a sign for a diner on the walk to the hotel.

* * * *

"Gunner. Hold up, man. What the fuck was that all about?" Hawk jogged toward his friend hell-bent on getting inside the building in under two seconds.

As soon as he stepped into the clubhouse, Hawk spotted Gunner making a beeline toward the bar.

"Shiiiit," he muttered, dragging the word out.

What the hell got him so pissed when he'd been about to give the woman a Gunner kiss to end all kisses? He hadn't seen his friend that upset since...

Since Peggy had died. He needed to find out just what had set him off. It had taken Gunner nearly a year to be able to function and another year to be able to control the anger inside of him. If their new president hadn't already had the name Rage, he'd have changed Gunner's to that almost immediately. The man had torn apart his place and started working on the club until Hawk and the brothers had stopped him.

"Gunner? What's going through your head right now? Talk to me." Hawk sat on the stool next to his friend and waited.

And waited.

"She's bad news. That's all. Don't know what I was thinking," he said, turning up the shot of whiskey one of the sweet butts had poured for him.

"Yeah, well. Most women are. What was different about this one?"

"Nothing. Just realized I was about to screw the pooch, and it pissed me off." He downed the next shot of whiskey, making a face as he slammed the glass down on the scarred bar.

Hawk knew his friend was lying to him about something but wasn't sure what it was. He didn't want to set him off over nothing, so he remained quiet, nursing his whiskey instead of downing it. Something about the woman that the other man had seen had caused the sudden turnaround in his mood and behavior. He just wasn't sure what it could have been.

"Hey, man. That bitch meant business. How come the punch didn't get you?" Jinx one of the other members of The Howling Death MC asked with a chuckle.

"Lay off the names, Jinx," Gunner muttered. "The punch hit my fucking piece, or I'd be laid up in the meat house with a fucking pipe in my chest. Figured it would have punctured my lung."

"And you don't like me calling her a bitch?" Jinx asked, his eyes wide in disbelief.

Hawk butted in so Gunner wouldn't lose it again. "She was scared to death of us, man. Can't blame the woman for trying to defend herself. Not all MCs are decent enough not to take advantage of a woman on her own like that."

"Okay, guess you're right. Hell, Gun. Glad you didn't have my luck. If it had been me, she probably would have gotten me in the heart." Jinx wandered off to harass one of the sweet butts gathering trash.

"Asshole," Gunner said under his breath.

"Think the parts house Terror is setting up will be a good investment?" Hawk asked his friend, hoping to change the subject to something less volatile.

"Yeah, actually I do. There isn't one within forty or so miles in any direction. The farmers and mechanics have to order all their parts over the Internet which costs money in shipping and takes time. Should pretty much break even until the loan's paid out," Gunner said, swirling the third shot of whiskey in the glass without downing it.

"That's all we can ask. The crew's pretty much flush for at least a couple of years with the bar and the gym. If we can get the bike shop up and running along with the parts store, maybe we can completely get out of the shady areas once and for all." Hawk sure hoped so. It was only a matter of time before something backfired on them. Times were different now.

Making the changes to keep them out of trouble was one of the reasons he liked Terror and Rage. He'd had to run the local chapter of The Howling Death MC once their previous officers had been killed. He wasn't a leader and had finally contacted the Mother chapter for help. When they'd sent Terror and Rage, nomads of the MC, he'd been worried. They'd looked like stone-cold killers, but turned out to be intelligent, coolheaded, and awesome leaders. He'd quickly gained respect for them and supported all their decisions and changes.

"Who's going to manage the parts house? I know Bush is going to run the front part, but someone has to handle the books and the inventory," Gunner said out of the blue.

"Loco's the best choice for that since he already handles the information and Bush would be good, too. He's familiar with handling our books as the secretary," Hawk suggested.

"Loco's already said he didn't have time with keeping all of our various interests kosher with law enforcement. Don't know about Bush. He's great with the books, but can't remember to order the fucking beer or toilet tissue worth shit. Got to have someone who knows parts and can stay on top of it without tying up money in inventory we don't need."

"True. Still can't believe we ended up without a single roll of toilet paper but had five cases of fucking paper towels. I'd swear he did it on purpose except he was the one stuck in the shitter yelling for someone to bring him something to wipe his ass," Hawk said with a chuckle.

"Well, one thing I can say about him. He learned to keep us stocked in bathroom supplies. I just think that having an abundance of poop paper doesn't compare to the cost of keeping a hundred more batteries than we need. What about the prospect?"

"Scooby's a damn good prospect and can follow directions better than most of us do, but he's no mechanic. Has to have help cleaning and taking care of his piece of shit bike as it is. He's out."

Gunner turned up the rest of the whiskey before slamming the shot glass upside down on the bar. The waitress picked it up and wiped the bar before setting the glass on a tray to be washed.

"That leaves you, Cowboy, and Jinx," Gunner drawled. "Think you can handle a regular job on top of security?"

"I'm not much better than Bush when it comes to knowing how much to order and when to do it. I can work the front when they need me to, and I plan to work in the bike shop, but I'm no inventory person." Hawk resisted the urge to gag at the idea of sitting inside behind a desk all the time. It was the one thing about going legit that bothered him. They weren't nine-to-five office types. They were bikers, use to the open road and causing mayhem.

"Wonder if old Hank was able to tow the lady's truck in and fix it?"

Hawk stared at Gunner before shaking his head. He smelled trouble.

Chapter Three

"Eight hundred dollars? Are you kidding me? That's highway robbery!" Jackie pulled at her hair in frustration.

"Yes, ma'am. That's about the size of it. The radiator is shot. There were two large holes, and one corner area was about to go, as well. I'm going to have to put in a new radiator, the hose, and a new bracket 'cause one of them is about to fall off from rust where the radiator's been leaking for Lord knows how long," the old man said.

"A damn radiator for the truck shouldn't be over two hundred, two hundred fifty dollars. The hose and bracket would be what?" She rubbed her forehead. "Maybe another one fifty at the most. Get me the fucking parts, and I'll do the work myself. I'm not paying four hundred dollars in labor. What are you doing, trying to pad your retirement fund?"

"T'aint that, lady. I have to order them parts, and the shipping is what drives the price up. We don't have no parts store within almost two hour's drive here. Them bikers are putting one in, but ain't open yet." He grimaced and shook his head. "I'll call around to see if I can find a used radiator and get it shipped, but that takes time, and I doubt you'll save more than fifty or sixty dollars on it."

"I don't believe it. How long before you can get the parts in?" Jackie asked in exasperation.

She was going to have to find a job somewhere in this hellhole to make enough money to pay for all of it. All she had to her name was the truck, her stuff, and about hundred and eighty dollars. With food and the motel room, that wouldn't last long at all. She'd probably need to sleep in her truck from now on.

"Figure if I get the parts new I can get them here in another two days with rush delivery. Of course that'll cost more. Otherwise, it will be three to four days depending on the weekend."

"Ah, hell. Order the parts but don't put the rush on it. I don't have enough money now as it is. I'm going to have to find a temporary job to pay you," she said.

"Got it, but I've got to have at least three hundred to order them." When she opened her mouth to protest he held up his hands. "Sorry, lady but that's how it is."

"I don't have that much. Will you at least let my truck stay parked outside the garage until I can get you the money?" she asked.

"Sure thing, hon. I'll park it right over there next to the scrap heap. Guy won't be around to pick it all up until first of the month anyway. You just let me know when you have the money and I'll order them parts for you." He smiled and left her standing in the gravel lot staring at her truck.

I guess things were going just a little too smoothly after all. Funny that being abducted by bikers was still too easy for me that I'm going to have to deal with finding a job to pay an arm and a leg just to be able to drive out of this place.

Where in the world was she going to find a job in a place like this? There was the diner, the motel, a general store of some type, a hardware slash feed store, and a bar. The motel wasn't going to need anyone, and the diner looked well-staffed, but she'd check and see anyway. The one thing she didn't want to have to do was waitress at a bar. Knowing her luck, that was exactly what it would come down to.

Jackie wasn't about to take a chance that she'd miss something, so she hit all the other spots in town first. No one had an opening. The bulletin board at the general store that also served as a grocer was empty of anything other than lost pets, equipment for sale, or AA and NA meeting schedules. That left the bar and her last chance at an easy way out of her troubles.

Hell, I've done worse things than parade around in tight jeans and a low-cut shirt to pay bills in the past.

"Pull up your big girl panties, Jackie and start walking."

From the outside, the place didn't look all that bad. The building had recently been painted and the sign that proclaimed it The Wagon Master Bar and Grill looked straight where it was mounted on the roof over the door. Music seeped through the small cracks around the door though there were only two trucks and a couple of bikes parked in the lot. Until that moment, Jackie hadn't considered that the guys from the day before might live in town. She'd figured they were passing through just like she'd been. But, they'd known there was a garage in town and what time it closed. They also knew where it was.

"They probably pass through town all the time on their way to and from whatever illegal shit they were into," she muttered as she stared once more at the dusty bikes.

She didn't recognize them, but then she hadn't actually been paying attention to what they'd been riding. All her attention had been on the ones doing the riding, that sexy voice and those well-defined muscular thighs.

God, don't get me started. I need to think about work and making enough money to fix my piece of shit truck. I don't have time for men or mayhem. It's all about the moola right now.

But that didn't make her feel any better. She'd shoved the experience all the way to the back of her brain where other less desirable memories lay and hadn't thought about it again. Yeah, her dreams had been filled with good-looking, rough around the edges smooth-talking men, but they hadn't worn leather vests or ridden motorcycles.

Only because they were in my bed and not wearing anything. The fact that there were two of them who looked like those two bikers doesn't count. I never really saw the one with the orgasm-generating voice anyway.

Jackie took one step in the direction of the door then looked down and adjusted the multiple leather and silicone support bands to be sure they hid the scars. Then she took another step and another until she'd reached the door. Just as she started to grab the doorknob, it swung open, and two burly looking men nearly knocked her over stomping out of the building.

"Whoa there, sweetheart. Sorry, didn't see you," one of the men said, sporting a slight beer belly and wearing a ball cap over what she was fairly sure was a bald head.

"No problem." She smiled and watched over her shoulder as they walked over to one of the dusty trucks and climbed in.

Crap, not the bikers. They're still in there.

Jackie drew in a deep breath then opened the door. She stepped inside and realized that the music was pretty low for a bar and, though it was a little dim in the huge room, she could see around her. The scent of cigarette smoke tickled her nose, but there wasn't enough in the air to be irritating. Most places didn't allow smoking inside now, but if this was a biker bar, no one was going to say anything about it.

Please don't belong to those bikers from yesterday.

A table near the back had been claimed by two men wearing leather vests leaning close to talk while they nursed their beers. Another man sat at the bar in the middle holding what she figured was a glass of whiskey between the palms of his hands. She didn't see anyone else in the room other than a hefty man that stood about six feet with a ponytail of brown hair and a short brown beard. He had a soft expression as he talked to one of the waitresses. Since he wasn't wearing a leather vest, Jackie held out some hope that it wasn't a biker bar after all.

She walked over to where the bartender leaned over the bar, listening to a short waitress with a head full of dirty blonde hair. Since it didn't appear to be about business, she cleared her throat, stopping just short of being within hearing distance of their obviously intimate conversation.

The man looked up with a smile and nodded. "What can I get you, honey?" he asked in a gruff voice.

The waitress remained sitting on the bar stool with her elbows on the bar on either side of her tray. She didn't look like a bar waitress. Her face had an almost angelic look to it with wide blue eyes and pouty pink lips. If she was even a day over eighteen, Jackie couldn't see it with binoculars. For one thing, she didn't have that certain "old" look around the eyes that hard living gives you almost at the beginning.

"Is the manager or the owner in?" she asked.

"Not the manager, hon, and the owners aren't here right now. What can I help you with?" he asked again.

"I'm looking for a job if you have an opening. I can tend bar, wait tables, cook, or wash dishes. Any chance you can give me a try?" she asked.

The waitress giggled then popped her hand over her mouth. Jackie frowned, knowing she had a puzzled look on her face, until it finally hit her what the girl was laughing about.

"Not give me a try that way," she said, rolling her eyes. "You know what I mean."

The big man just smiled and shook his head. "Yeah. I do. As it so happens, we do need a part-time waitress and a part-time cook. Probably not enough hours just working one way or the other. If you want to work both and Scoot, the manager, hires you, I can arrange some of the shifts that are open so you can cook then pull a few hours on the floor."

Despite usually keeping her feelings off her face, Jackie felt the relief of having a way to fix her immediate problem. Finally, something was going her way.

"What. The. Fuck!"

A voice from behind her shot that thought right out of the sky in a heartbeat.

* * * *

Gunner couldn't believe his eyes when he and Hawk walked into The Wagon Master after church that morning. His buddy ran into him from behind when he'd stopped midstride to stare at the hitchhiker from the day before. What the hell was she still doing in town?

"G, man? What the fuck?" Hawk stepped around him but stopped whatever he'd been about to say when he caught sight of the girl.

"I thought you'd be long gone from here by now," he snapped as he strode to where she stood glaring at him like he'd done something to her.

"Truck needs a radiator then I'll be back on the road," she snarled back.

"Not soon enough," he mumbled under his breath before slapping his hand on the bar a few feet down from where she leaned against the bar. "Duke, two beers."

Turning his back to her, he nodded at Hawk and walked to the back where Cowboy and Jinx nursed their drinks. He jerked out one of the chairs and turned it around to straddle it. Hawk took the one to the right of him and plopped down without a word. Gunner could hear the questions boiling in the back of his friend's head, though. Hawk didn't let anything get by him.

"Cowboy, Jinx. Hear any more talk about the problem with the One-Niners?" he asked his fellow brothers.

"Nothing yet," Cowboy said. "We were just talking about how the bastards just disappeared off the radar. I'd almost believe talk of them trying to cause trouble was just a rumor, except that stirring the pot is what they love to do."

"What it all comes down to is what's in it for them if they screw up our sanctuary plans. What do they stand to gain? Any ideas?" Hawk asked.

"Nope. Not yet." Jinx turned up his beer and sat back. "Do you think we've got too many irons in the fire, Hawk?"

Gunner stilled at the other man's comment. As vice president, Hawk held a good bit of power and information. It was saying something that Jinx felt comfortable enough to ask something like that without Terror or Rage present. Rage was the president of The Howling Death MC with his twin brother as his partner in the role.

"We're spreading it pretty thin, Jinx, but we've got new blood rolling in every day. If we don't get everything up and going as soon as possible, we're going to need a way to augment our finances." Hawk leaned forward, laying his forearms on the table. "And we all agreed we wanted out of the darker parts of the business."

"I agree," Jinx said. "I'm just worried with whatever is going on between the Vipers and the One-Niners is going to catch us with our pants down."

"Ever since Homeland pissed all over their weapons deal last year, the Vipers have been struggling to reform and regroup. Losing the top echelon of their leadership had effectively screwed them out of anything big enough to fund the MC. That means they've got something else going on we don't know about," Cowboy added.

"True, but we've got it covered. Is this something working around the club or just the two of you voicing your own ideas?" Gunner asked them.

Both men sat back slowly and flattened their hands on the table. He realized his edgy side had come out when he'd seen the woman he'd wanted to forget about standing at the bar. He needed to tone it down some before he said or did something he couldn't take back.

"Some of the guys are concerned, but no one is complaining. It's not anything that's a problem, Gunner," Jinx told him in a low, clear voice.

"Good. Maybe we should have a town hall meeting with everyone and talk about it," Hawk suggested, looking at Gunner as he said it.

"Sounds like a good idea," Gunner agreed.

"Here you go, guys." Duke set their beer in front of them and exchanged Jinx's and Cowboy's for fresh ones, as well. "Is Scoot going to be by this afternoon?"

"Said he's planning to come in around seven. Why? Problem?" Hawk asked.

"No. Got someone wanting the waitress and cook jobs. Didn't know whether to have her stick around or come back," he said.

Gunner's pulse stuttered. Did he fucking mean the woman he'd just spoken to? He turned around to stare at the sinfully sexy one talking with Trish. Looking around, he realized there wasn't another female in the room. Unless she'd hit the john while Duke brought over their beers, the woman he'd been trying to forget about was the one the bartender was referring to.

Well, fuck me.

"That her?" Hawk asked, nodding at the same one Gunner stared at.

"Yep, name's Jack, short for Jackie. Got experience in everything including bartending, so she's perfect to fill all the part-time slots we can't fill," Duke told them.

"Why hire her when she's not sticking around?" he asked.

"None of them stay for long, Gunner. Help now is better than no help now." Hawk stared hard at him. "What is it about her that pisses you off, man?"

"Nothing." He stood and turned the chair back around to face the table. "I'll go call Scoot to get him on out here."

Duke exchanged looks with the other guys before returning to the bar to talk to the broad. What had he said her name was? Jack-Jackie? What kind of name was that for a woman anyway?

Hawk just nodded but didn't say anything. Gunner knew he would have a lot to answer for when they were out of earshot of anyone else. Couldn't really blame the man. He was the vice president as well as his best friend. He owed the man respect as well as an explanation for his shitty attitude.

Gunner walked across the room toward the door. The weight of her gaze was almost bruising as he stepped outside to make the call. It wasn't until the door slammed behind him that he was able to breathe without struggling. He refused to let it mean anything. Instead, he punched in Scoot's number and waited while it rang then went to voice mail.

Gunner left a brief message then ended the call with a low growl. Going back inside meant awareness that she would still be there, waiting to talk to Scoot. He'd gotten close enough when he'd first arrived to find out that her light brown eyes reminded him of doe eyes. Her shaggy, kind of screwed-up hair fell just past her shoulders in a variegated rainbow of rich browns and lighter shades that gave it a sun-streaked look.

And there he was thinking about her when he should have been forgetting all about her after seeing the scars on her wrists. The first thing he'd looked for when he realized it was her at the bar had been her wrists. He'd noticed that she'd covered them with those silicone remembrance bracelets as well as a wide leather one on her right wrist.

He paced back and forth at a slow clip as he thought about her comment and the news that she was looking for a job. She obviously needed the money to fix that heap of shit she'd had to have towed in. The best way to settle everything would be to pay to get the truck fixed so she could get out of town and out of his head. He didn't need the distraction with everything the MC had going on at the moment. Just knowing she was in town would screw with his head if he let it and at the moment, he didn't have a lot of leftover energy to keep it out.

"Fuck!"

It wasn't her dangerous curves or thoughts of those thick muscular thighs wrapped around his waist that held his attention. He wasn't focused on how delicious her tits looked smashed against his partner's back. It was those damn scars. They pissed him off. He couldn't interfere with Scoot's business as the manager of the bar no matter how much he wanted to ask the man to refuse to hire her.

Since they'd bought the owners out when they'd decided to retire to Las Vegas, finding enough help had become an issue. They needed the help. Bad. But if she didn't need the money, she wouldn't stick around so his paying for the repairs wouldn't exactly be interfering. She didn't have to leave if she didn't want to, right?

No matter how he looked at it, though, there just wasn't another option. Her sticking around for even a few weeks was dangerous for his sanity, and with the shit getting deeper as they pushed forward with their plans to make Settler's Point a sort of biker sanctuary, keeping his head where it needed to be was imperative.

She had to go.

Chapter Four

Her nemesis crossed the bar in long strides, reaching the door and shoving through it before Jackie had enough time to appreciate his tight ass that flexed with each movement in well-worn tight jeans. Despite his asshole attitude, she couldn't help but admire the man's exceptionally honed body.

I need someone to remind me why I am where I am right now because I must have forgotten the last ten years of my freakish life.

As soon as he'd let the door slam behind him, Jackie slid her gaze toward the back table once more. There, without his helmet to hide his face had to be the sexy-talking biker she'd ridden behind. Between the vibrations of the bike between her legs, the feel of his hard abdomen beneath her hands, and the memory of his deep, panty-drenching voice, she'd had one hell of a fantasy while she'd showered the night before. That had been followed by her sexy ménage dream later that night.

She'd caught a brief flash of the mystery biker's face when they'd first walked in, but his bastard of a friend had gotten in the way, and by the time he'd walked away, his friend was already past and taking a seat in the back. Now all she could see was the side view of him. Not that she'd complain. He had a nice one.

She was pretty sure she'd seen dark eyes, and she could still tell that he had dark brown hair cut in a shaggy style that just barely curled at his shoulder. He was shorter than his friend, maybe six feet to the other man's six-three. They both seemed to have the same aversion to shaving, since both men still had scruffy faces.

But, Jackie didn't mind the scruff, it was the first guy's attitude that sucked. One minute he'd acted like he was going to kiss her then he'd taken one look at her scars and changed his stripes. Evidently he was one of those black and white people who didn't see the shades of gray in between. It was kind of hypocritical to her considering his lifestyle as a biker. Of course, she was straying from her gray area into that "it's either black or it's white" group if she pointed out his obvious appearance.

I just need to stop it already. Land this job or jobs, and pay to have my truck fixed so I can get back on the road.

On the road to where, though? She still hadn't fleshed out that part of her great plan to start over. Jackie was just proud of herself for putting the plan into motion and leaving. She could worry about where she would end up later.

The sound of the door slamming again jerked her thoughts back to the bar, the glass of water she'd asked for sitting in front of her, and the feel of someone's focused stare on her back. Jackie resisted the need to turn and see who it was. She was already pretty certain it would be bad biker boy. She expected him to walk past her to the table where his friends were, so when a hand appeared next to hers on the bar, all the air in her lungs evaporated even as all of it around her disappeared.

"We need to talk."

His words right next to her ear caused her to shiver, and suddenly she could breathe again.

What the hell just happened?

"What about?" Her voice came out husky instead of uninterested like she'd planned.

"Your truck and what you need to fix it," he whispered close to her shoulder.

"W—what are you talking about?"

"Fixing your truck so you can be on your way. That's what's keeping you here isn't it?"

Suddenly Jackie's body felt as if menopause had claimed its next victim with a vengeance. Why had it chosen her when she was barely twenty-nine? She was sure her neck and face had turned blood-red by the heat that radiated off her skin.

"Don't worry. As soon as I earn the money to fix it, I'm out of here." Now, why had she told him that? Why did it matter to him if she stuck around or not?

"How much?" he asked, leaning closer to her. He seemed to be putting all his weight on the hand next to hers on the bar, since it had turned red except for his fingertips and the creases at the wrist that were now white.

"How much for what?"

"To fix that miserable excuse for a truck. How much is it going to cost to get you back on the road?" he asked again.

Jackie had to think about taking the next breath and the one after that. Something about how he stood over her, crowding into her from behind, drugged her and took away her reasoning ability. Had the heat burning her skin boiled her brain as well? If she hadn't been consciously controlling her breathing, Jackie was sure she'd have passed out by now. They were in a world of only two, and nothing else mattered around them. He sucked in her oxygen, and she fought to find more.

"Eight hundred dollars," she finally told him.

Their little world popped when he said something so obviously made up that even her colorful language couldn't have competed. She pulled away from him, redefining her space.

"I thought you said it was a busted radiator. What the hell else is he doing, lining it with gold?"

Jackie told herself not to turn around, but she never was one to take her own advice. The instant she did, she regretted it. Hot eyes, dark as sin, glared at her as if she'd purposefully put the hole in her own radiator just to piss him off. The scowl that drew his brows together into a single line didn't worry her. It just added fuel to her already stoked anger.

"Don't yell at me, asshole. It's your damn town that's gouging visitors with jacked-up prices and sob stories. If I could get the fucking parts I could fix it myself, so back the hell off, biker boy!" She knew better, but she poked her finger in his chest twice then turned her back and grabbed the glass of water off the bar to ease the tightness in her throat.

"I'll pay for the work on your truck. All you have to do is leave as soon as it's finished."

Had she heard him right? Jackie wasn't sure. She slowly turned to face him, swallowing down all the emotion boiling in her chest until it rested in the pit of her stomach to roll some more.

"What did you say?" Her voice sounded soft and steady even to her.

He hesitated for all of a second. "I said I'd pay for the repairs."

"As long as I leave as soon as it's ready," she finished.

"Yeah."

She drew in a slow breath then let it seep out of her skin before answering him with a smile.

"No."

* * * *

"Duke said you were interested in working both jobs. Said you have experience, that right?" Scoot, the bar's manager shifted in his seat behind the dented metal desk.

"That's right. I've worked every position in a bar and a restaurant at one time or another. I don't mind hard work or long hours. I just need the money to fix my truck," she told him.

"I see. So you're not planning to stick around?"

It was a trick question. She was sure of it. He wore the same leather vest that her nemesis and the other guys had on, so she was positive he'd already had a conversation with a certain pissed-off biker before he'd joined her in the office. If she said no, he could decide not to hire her. If she said she would stick around for a while, he might not because of the asshole biker.

"I can't very well go anywhere without my wheels. I won't leave you hanging. I promise." She settled on evasive honesty. It usually got her by.

Scoot nodded but didn't say anything for a few seconds. Then he leaned back in the chair and ran a hand over his face, stopping to pull at the short goatee that looked like the only beard he could manage to grow. Scraggly didn't even begin to cover it. It looked more like a rat's tail that should have been on the back of his head instead of on his chin.

"Got legal ID?" he finally asked.

"Yeah."

Relief trickled down her spine like the sweat that had already made that same trip several times now. Jackie pulled her wallet out of the backpack she'd sat on the floor by the chair. Sliding out her driver's license and Social cards, she held them out to the man.

He took them before pulling out a drawer that made a god-awful racket and digging through some folders. Tossing a form down on the desk in front of her, Scoot got up and walked the two steps it took to get to the primeval—or maybe prehistoric was the right word?—dirty copier sitting on top of an equally ancient metal file cabinet. He had to slide a blade across the paper when it had finished printing.

"Fill that out, and you can start tomorrow at three. You'll cook till nine then wait tables till close. Can you handle that?" he asked before handing her cards back across the desk.

"No problem. Thanks for giving me a chance."

He sighed and shook his head. "Don't thank me yet. This isn't going to be an easy job. Place fills up early and doesn't let up till we kick them out around two. If you make it tomorrow, we'll look at the schedule."

"I'll make it. I've worked in worse, I promise you." She quickly filled out the paperwork, putting the hotel down as her address even though she didn't know what it was, and made a mental note to get a prepaid phone and give Scoot the number when she came back in the next afternoon.

"Do us both a favor and avoid Gunner, will you?"

"Who?" She had a sinking feeling he was referring to biker boy, though.

"The guy who wants you gone. I don't know what your history is and don't give a flying fuck, but I'm still here when you're nothing but exhaust fumes. If I didn't need the help so fucking badly, I wouldn't hire you. Remember that if you get a wild hair to do something stupid like piss in his beer or spit on his burger, got it?"

"Yeah. I've got it." She shoved the paper and pen across the desk and stood, picking her pack up off the floor as she did.

Without a second glance at the man who'd simultaneously answered her prayers and kicked her puppy, Jackie opened the door and walked out without closing it behind her. She pulled the pack's strap over one shoulder and made a beeline to the door. Since she'd been in the office, at least a dozen or more customers had settled at various tables, the noise level already twice as loud as when she'd first walked into the wide-open room. Despite the burning knife she could feel digging into her back from someone's stare behind her, Jackie didn't spare a single glance in the direction of the table of bikers in the back. She didn't even know if he was still back there, nor did she care.

The second she'd cleared the door, Jackie felt pounds lighter. Once she'd put a couple hundred yards between her and the bar, she was able to breathe normally and nearly forget the feel of Gunner's heated breath against her skin. Almost. The lingering pressure that had teased her body while he'd had her caged against the bar wouldn't let her get by that easily, though. If she let her guard down, it all rolled back over her like a bulldozer, piling it all right back on top of her as if it had never been gone at all.

What is it about him that pisses me off and makes me want to lick every inch of his skin at the same time? He's an asshole. I shouldn't even care that he is.

Jackie stopped just outside the office of the motel and thought about it for a second. Was she angry that he'd offered to pay to have her truck fixed just to get her out of his hair or was she angry that her scars mattered to him for some reason?

"Why do I care either way? To care implies that his opinion matters to me and it doesn't."

It really doesn't.

"You talk to yourself lot?"

Jackie jumped then smiled as the tiny old Asian woman shuffled down the walkway and opened the door to go inside. The woman probably thought she was one or two noodles shy of a full brick of Ramon noodles.

She slipped into the office behind the woman and stood at the desk to wait for the elderly lady to walk around the side to greet her. She looked up at Jackie and smiled so big it looked like it should hurt.

"You stay more, or you check out now?"

"I stay, um, I need to rent the room for a few weeks if that's okay."

"Rent by night or by month. Don't do hourly, got it?" she asked.

"Yeah. Don't worry. I don't do hourly, either. So how much for a month?" She truly didn't want to stay that long, but depending on how long it took her to make what she needed, she'd cut her losses and leave as soon as the truck was fixed regardless of where she was in the month.

"One thousand for month. Includes weekly room change. You put garbage in bag in Dumpster in between," she said, showing the pearly white but crooked teeth with her dangerously wide smile again.

"If I rent it for the month, can I pay you by the week? I only have enough for one week until I get paid."

"How you get paid with no job?" the woman asked, her brows lifting high enough to disappear into her hair.

"I'm working at The Wagon Master Bar and Grill. I start tomorrow afternoon," she told her with a smug smile.

The elderly woman narrowed her eyes before answering. "No visitors in room and no loud bikes in parking lot. I let you pay end of each week. You already paid two nights of month's rent. You make noise and you go."

Jackie couldn't decide whether to be insulted or laugh. She was tough but smart and just as cute in her own Hannibal smile way.

"Thanks." She almost chuckled when her landlady huffed then turned and left her standing there.

Fifteen minutes and one vending machine trip later, she sat on the bed in her room drinking a Diet Sprite because that was all that was in the machine and eating a mixture of crunchy Cheetos, peanut butter crackers, and a honeybun for dessert. It wasn't nutritious or even good, but it stopped the gnawing pain in her belly and didn't require walking to and from the store with a load of groceries. She'd make that trip tomorrow before work.

Right then, all she wanted to do was soak her sore feet in preparation for being on them all night when she got to work the next day. Why hadn't she thought to buy a pair of sneakers while she'd been out? Waiting tables and short order cooking in boots wouldn't be easy, and when she pulled them off to go to bed, it would probably be more along the line of pure hell.

"Better add Band-Aids and Epsom salts to the list, as well. I'm going to need a damn truck to get everything. Too bad mine's in the shop."

Jackie snorted and crumbled up all the wrappers from her meal. She scooted to the edge of the bed and tossed the expanding ball at the garbage can, missing it by a good foot. She would pick it up later. Right then all she wanted to do was take a nap that would lead into going to bed for the night. And while she was making plans, she planned not to dream about two leather-clad bikers with howling wolves on their leather vests.

Chapter Five

"Spit it out, Gunner. What the fuck is going on between you and that woman, what's her name, Jackie, right?"

Hawk wanted to knock some sense into the other man, but that was more Gunner's style, not his. Or least it hadn't been until they'd picked up a certain hitchhiker. Now Hawk wanted to bring some violence down on his best friend. What was it that had gotten under the other man's skin? She'd ridden on the back of Hawk's bike, not Gunner's, so nothing had happened on the ride into town. The other man had been all about trash talking as they carried her to the garage. Somewhere between the time Gunner had gotten off his bike and helped their hitchhiker off Hawk's, something had happened that had turned his friend from a smooth-talking Valentino to Dr. Jekyll's Mr. Hyde.

"Nothing's going on with her." He stared at Hawk for a second. "She just rubs me the wrong way, and I sure as hell don't need the distraction with everything going on right now."

"That's right, you don't, but don't give me some bullshit about her rubbing you the wrong way. The way you were talking on the ride after we picked her up, you were planning on having her rub on you in a different way. What happened? Did she say something I didn't hear or do something I didn't see?"

"No! I told you there's nothing to it. I just don't like her. Now don't fucking bring it up again." Gunner jammed his helmet on and started his bike, slinging gravel as he tore out of the parking lot.

"Nothing my ass."

Hawk pulled out of the lot at a slower pace than his buddy had. He thought over when they'd stopped at the garage to let the woman off to what had happened. Normally he could recall events in detail without having to think about it, but he'd already been thinking about what needed to be done to get ready for the parts store's grand opening in a month. He'd seen Gunner's slow smile as he helped her off the back of his bike and knew from experience what he was up to. After that, Hawk had tuned it all out and went over the list in his head again to make sure he hadn't missed something.

The next thing he'd known, Gunner was walking away from the woman with a disgusted expression Hawk hadn't seen since one of the parties they'd been invited to at a sister club out in Vegas on one of their trips. It had all started out just like any biker bonfire with drinking, smoking a little weed, and getting it on with sweet butts. Next thing they knew, several of the guys from the host club were pissing all over some of the women like fucking dogs. He'd seen a perfect description of what he felt on his friend's face, and they'd made it an early night.

It still made him gag at the thought of treating a woman that way. Sweet butts might be mutual property, but they were still women and could walk out anytime they wanted to. Gunner seemed to think that those women hadn't really had that option. They weren't attending any future events of that club that was for damn sure.

What about Jackie could possibly have put that look on Gunner's face again? She seemed nice enough from the few minutes he'd known her. She hadn't acted turned off by their being bikers, only cautious and maybe a little afraid.

I don't know what's going on, but I'm sure as hell going to find out before Gunner gets himself hurt or, worse, all of us in trouble if his head isn't in the game.

He'd have a talk with Scoot tomorrow after Jackie had worked a few hours to see if the other man noticed anything strange about her. When he'd finished talking to her and she'd left, Hawk had asked him what he thought about the woman. All he'd said was that she seemed smart and very confident she could handle the jobs.

If that didn't shake something loose, he'd have a talk with her. Worse came to worse, he'd have to go to the prez over it and see what he wanted to do. Hawk didn't want it to get that far, but Gunner's sanity and the club's well-being came first. His friend would be pissed off and either beat the fuck out of him or give him the silent treatment for a while—then it would all blow over. Still, Hawk didn't like hammering away on the trust they had for each other.

When he rode down the single-lane road leading to their clubhouse, he prayed Gunner was there and hadn't gone off riding at three in the morning by himself. Wasn't safe for any of them to go off alone these days and definitely not at night. To his relief, his cycle was parked in the normal spot. Hawk waved at one of the prospects standing near the bikes as guard for the night.

The clubhouse looked a hell of a lot better than it had when they'd lost half their members in an all-out war several years back. Terror and Rage were good for the club and had solid ideas to keep them pretty much on the straight and narrow. So far, they'd bought the bar, were in partners with Bear at the gym, were opening a parts store, and were expanding the bike shop to include custom work and hot rod repairs.

Along with that and working toward setting Settler's Point up as a sanctuary, they'd managed to enlarge the clubhouse and update everything, so it was comfortable with several small suites for out of town guests and when a brother needed to stay overnight. They encouraged all the club members to buy or build houses in the area instead of bunking at the clubhouse all the time.

Rage said it showed a commitment to the community and would gain them respect as contributing to the town instead of respect out of the fear. Some of the guys didn't much care how they got their respect, but as he'd gotten older, the looks he used to get from people made his soul tired.

"What's crawled up Gunner's ass?" Loco asked as soon as he walked into the community room.

"Don't know. Why?" He ran his hands through his hair to rake it down after pulling off the helmet.

"Stomped through here like a damn bear then roared at KK when she asked if he wanted some company." Loco pulled KK closer and kissed her cheek.

"He'll settle down. Everything's up in the air right now with the plans and now talk about the One-Niners. Cut him some slack for a few days."

He sure as fuck better settle down, or I'm going beat the reason for his attitude right out of him.

"Why the hell would he be worried about those mothers?"

"It's just one more brick in the wall, Loco. It's all good." Hawk bumped fists with him before walking toward the kitchen.

As soon as he entered the room, Hawk stopped dead in his tracks.

* * * *

Gunner heard someone walk into the kitchen but didn't bother to look up. Instead, he filled his glass from the half-empty bottle again and turned it up. It burned nice and sweet going down, hitting his stomach with a punch that warned him he'd regret this later. He didn't give a rat's ass about later. Later might never come. Right then all he wanted was to feel warm again. He needed the cold, the bitter arctic chill that had razor sharp claws cutting into his soul to just be gone. Completely, entirely gone for good.

"You just left a bar, and now you're going to start drinking again?" The anger in Hawk's voice didn't bother him in the least at the moment.

"Couldn't get a good buzz on when I had to drive back here, now could I?" He poured another glass of whiskey, not bothering to cap the bottle afterward. He was only going to have to take it back off again in a minute.

"I'm not your fucking mother or your priest, so I'm not going to lecture you, Gunner..." he began.

"Then don't! Shut the hell up and keep on walking."

"But drinking isn't going to solve whatever has your britches twisted, man. You know that."

Gunner grabbed the bottle, thinking briefly about throwing it at the man but thought better of it. No reason to waste perfectly good booze on the asshole, no matter how pissed he was. He just wanted the fucking memories to disappear and take that damn woman with them.

Why? Why did she have to show up in this town of all the shitholes in the state when he was just starting to stop remembering? Why did it even matter in the first place? She was nothing to him. Once she earned enough to pay for the repairs on her truck, she would be gone. Good fucking riddance.

"Don't shut me out, man. We've been through hell then dove into purgatory together. Spit it out and let's deal with it. What's wrong?" Hawk pulled out a chair and sat across the table.

Gunner sighed and capped the bottle. He wasn't going to be able to enjoy getting his drunk on anyway. Standing, he slid the bottle of numbing oblivion back into the cabinet and quietly shut the door. It took a few seconds for him to swallow down the pain, but once he'd managed, Gunner sat back down to look at his friend for nearly twenty-five years. They'd grown up together, hidden from their fucked-up dads together. They didn't keep secrets, but some things were just too painful to dredge up again.

He looked at his hands. He just couldn't look at the pity he knew he'd see in Hawk's eyes when he said it. He could handle just about anything, any emotion, any pain, any disappointment, but he couldn't handle the pity. Never had been able to even when he'd been a child.

"When I looked at her after she got off your bike at the garage, she reminded me of her. I'd been trash talking about the little hitchhiker all the way into town, wanting to mess around with her, see if I could talk her into sticking around for a while when it punched me in the gut. I just can't deal with it, Hawk." He fisted his hands over and over again, watching his knuckles grow white then blood-red.

"I don't understand, Gunner. She doesn't look one bit like Peggy. How could she remind you of her?" Hawk shifted in his chair.

"Her eyes. She had that same, almost dead look that used to tear me up every time I saw it. Always made me feel like a failure. Like I should have been able to do something." He looked away. "I just couldn't handle seeing that again."

"There was nothing you could do for her, man. We've been over it before. Peggy was always a little broken. Even before the miscarriages. You know that."

He finally looked up. "Doesn't make it right. I should have been there. I could have stopped her."

"Yeah, like you'd stopped her how many times before? There would always have been a next time and a next time until it happened and you were there. It was inevitable, Gunner." Hawk drew in a deep breath and leaned back in the chair. "I just wish we'd realized she was sick before things got serious between you."

"I knew what she was going to do, Hawk. I had a gut feeling, but I was tired of her games, and we were in the middle of a war that was about to come crashing down on us. I should have gone back instead of waiting." He shook his head and stood. "I'll see you in the morning."

Gunner walked out of the kitchen and down the hall that led to the old part of the clubhouse. It was where the guys slept or took the girls back for fun and games. He had no need for anything more than a bed and access to a toilet. All he wanted to do was sleep. No dreams, no nightmares, just sleep.

He chose the first room that had an open door. Checking to make sure the sheets had been changed, Gunner shut the door with the toe of his boot then locked it and grabbed the back of his T-shirt and pulled it over his head and off his arms before dropping it at his feet. He sat on the creaky bed and pulled off one boot then the other, letting them drop with a muted thump on the floor.

Her light brown eyes reminded him of a timid doe, suspicious of her surroundings. For a brief second, he'd seen arousal and maybe even a little bit of longing before the darkness, that pit of emptiness took over. That's when he'd known that she was just like his dead wife. One look at the scars on her wrists told him that he'd been right. Not again. Never again.

What the hell am I going to do with her working at the bar? I can't fucking avoid the place since we hang out there and talk most nights. I can't look at her and know what she's done and probably going to do again without it eating me up inside.

The real kicker was that he was attracted to her for some stupid reason. Something about the way she moved and the defiant way she'd tried to hide her fear drew him close. It made him want to wrap her in his arms to keep her safe then fuck her brains out to hear the wild screams he knew would be there. Only Gunner knew nothing he could do would ever keep her safe from herself. He couldn't hold her enough or love her enough to change whatever demons she fought deep down inside where no one else could touch but her.

He unfastened his belt and the top button of his jeans then stretched out on top of the covers with his hands clasped behind his head. No use in getting comfortable. He wouldn't be getting much sleep now.

Chapter Six

"Two burgers with the works and a large order of fries!" Jackie was going to hear that order in her dreams. It was just about the same order she'd gotten over and over again since she'd clocked in at three.

It was nearly six and her feet already burned from standing on hard concrete for three hours straight. She dreaded the next eight she still had to go. It was the fucking boots. If she'd had decent shoes with some cushion, it wouldn't be as bad. She swore that she would make sure and buy a pair before she returned to work.

So far, everything had gone smoothly. No one had complained about their order or how long they had to wait for it. It had been a good four years since she'd cooked short order, but it wasn't rocket science or fancy meals. She could handle flipping burgers and dropping fries. Waiting tables didn't bother her either. She could do that in her sleep no matter how busy they got.

No, it was Gunner, the guy who'd tried to buy her way out of town for her. Why hadn't she taken him up on the offer?

Because I don't take charity when I can earn what I need, and I sure as hell don't take handouts.

But Jackie knew she could have paid him back once she'd found a job in a different town. It had been his attitude that had pissed her off. She didn't follow orders from strangers who weren't her boss, and she absolutely didn't from sanctimonious bastards like a damn biker. What the hell was up with that, anyway?

She refused to allow even an inkling of the truth that she was attracted to the asshole figure into it. Jackie could admit to a little infatuation with his buddy, Mr. Sexy as Sin Voice. That she could accept, but not his royal ass-ness. He didn't figure into it one bit.

The snort escaped before she could stop it, eliciting a giggle before she realized her fries were going to burn if she didn't pull them up.

"Need another order of fries, Jack," Duke shouted through the opening.

It hadn't taken long for Duke and the other waitresses to accept her nickname. They got a kick out of using it, especially when she ended up taking the orders out herself so they wouldn't get cold waiting for one of them to have time to take the meal to the table. The customers checked out the name tag on her shirt twice before giving her a long, puzzled look.

She'd told one table that she was just filling in for Jack and using his shirt. She was fairly sure they had believed her. Chrissy, one of the waitresses, had laughed and slapped her on the back before telling the others what she'd done.

"You're going to fit in here just fine, Jack," Duke had said. "Just keep away from Gunner and everything will be good."

"Right," she muttered under her breath after returning to the kitchen. "And I'm the Easter Bunny."

She had a short lull before eight. Jackie cleaned the kitchen so she wouldn't have as much to do later. While she worked, she tried to make plans for when her truck was ready. She wanted to eventually make it to Farmington, Missouri. A distant relative on her mom's side lived there. Her mom had always talked about how much she missed her aunt Beany. They'd called her that when they hadn't been able to pronounce her real name, Beatrice. At four and five years of age, Beany's name stuck until she moved away to get married.

Her mom said Aunt Beany would come back to visit until Mom had married Joe. Then after a few years, she didn't come back. Mom had told her that Dad hated Beany because she fussed at him all the time. Beany hadn't approved of the way Joe treated them. Jackie could easily attest to that. He'd been a mean drunk and a poor provider. Half the time it was her mom who'd worked to put food on the table, which meant she and her siblings were home alone with their dad all day.

Jackie could remember very little about her aunt since she'd only been about five when there'd been that big fight. Her dad had told Aunt Beany never to come back, or he'd make her sorry. She remembered her mom begging her aunt just to go so there wouldn't be any trouble. And she'd gone. As far as Jackie knew, her mom had never talked to her again, though there had been a few letters here and there. Jackie and the others tried to catch the mailman before her dad so they could hide anything that was addressed to their mom.

The memories burned in her gut just like always, but they were nowhere near as hard to live with as the ones that came later. Those she kept under lock and key. Those had no room in her world anymore. She was starting over, without those terrible secrets to pull her down.

She didn't plan on staying with her aunt Beany. Jackie just wanted to see her again. Maybe just to prove that there had been someone who had loved them back then when it didn't feel like there was anyone who cared. Her mom had believed that everything would get better one day. She'd believed it right up until the end, when Jackie's dad had finally snapped and gone on a shooting spree.

Jackie looked down and realized she'd been drying the same spatula for the last few minutes. She hated it when she got lost in the memories. They didn't do her any good. She needed to forget it all and stop going back through them like picture albums. All it did was reopen old wounds. Old wounds that didn't heal led to infections that slowly ate away at you from the inside until it was too late to get anything that would heal them.

"Hey, Jack! I'm going to close the kitchen down a little early tonight. We're swamped out here. Go ahead and shut everything down and help wait tables. They can live without their burgers and fries, but they can't live without their booze." Duke's chuckle reminded her that she was alive and living a new life.

"Be right there." Jackie quickly double-checked the fryers and the grill then locked the padlocks on the freezer and fridge.

By the time she'd changed from her full apron to the shorter one, she could hear the increasing noise level as people crowded in to visit, listen to music, and drink, not necessarily in that order.

"Where do you want me?" she asked, Duke.

"Help me behind here for now. I can't keep the trays filled and handle the bar at the same time. Don't know what the hell is going on in town, but someone left the gate open."

Jackie laughed and got to work. When shift change came at nine, she was exhausted and still had another five or so hours to go. She could already feel the blisters on her feet and figured there would be even more before she made it back to the hotel.

"Jack, this is Gail. She'll show you your section and fill you in. I've got to leave it with you until Randy gets here. Then you can let him take over, and you can hit the floor. Great working with ya', kid." Duke gave her a soft punch in the arm and pulled off the bar apron he wore to step down and walk toward the back of the room where the rest of his club sat talking.

"Jack?" Gail asked with a raised brow. "How'd you end up with that name?"

"Name's Jackie, but it gets shortened to Jack all the time. Doesn't bother me, though." She shrugged. "Okay, what do you need?"

* * * *

Gunner swung his leg over the back of the bike and pulled off his helmet. He'd put off coming for as long as he could. Hawk had made him promise he'd show up before ten and he had. Twice now. It was a quarter of and this was it. He couldn't pass the place by one more time.

Never in his adult life had he ever felt this uneasy about something. Even all the years the club had been into some nasty shit he hadn't known a moment's fear. There'd been days he'd dreaded what was coming or had known it was going to be bad, but fear hadn't entered into it. Not once.

Well it did now.

If he hadn't been attracted to the woman, Gunner was certain it wouldn't have given him a moment's hesitation. He'd have shaken his head, hated that someone felt that desperate then gone on with his life without it cutting into him like it did. The problem was that he liked what he saw with her curvy, wide ass and those mounds of happiness sitting on her chest. He knew she'd be soft and comfortable in his arms and beneath his head.

The way she moved had nearly mesmerized him, and the sight of her wrapped around Hawk on the back of the bike had nearly caused him to come in his jeans. He'd always admired strength, and even though she'd been nervous and a little afraid, she'd remained calm and tried to stand her ground. She'd even surrendered with an air of control. It had fascinated and drawn him to her like a bear to a beehive. Only her sting had been much too close to home for him.

The instant he stepped inside the dim building, Gunner was aware of her. It was as if the noise of the rowdy crowd and the ringing of the amplifiers from the stage receded and all he could see and feel was Jackie.

Fuuuck!

It was too late to turn around and leave, Hawk and Rage were already making their way toward him. Gunner forced a relaxed expression on even though he felt far from relaxed. Not only did he need a drink but a good hand job would be just as welcome.

Hell. I'd probably lose the wood if someone else touched me. I'm so fucked.

How could she arouse him just by being in the same room despite what she represented to him?

"Wasn't sure you were going to show up." Rage stopped right in front of him. "We've got some intel on the One-Niners. You solid?"

Gunner jerked his gaze over to Hawk, making sure the man who was supposed to be his best friend saw how irritated he was that the other man had said something to the prez. Didn't matter that it was his job as vice prez to keep Rage and Terror informed. But he wasn't losing it. He wouldn't put his brothers in danger.

"Don't piss on him over this, G-man. This is too fucking serious to risk everything because someone reminds you of your ex. If that's all it is, just get over it, man. Fuck her and get her out of your system."

As if that's all it would take. The way I feel right now, sex with her would just seal the deal. No. Hell. No.

"I'm good. Let's go." Gunner glared one last time at Hawk, showing the other man his teeth then followed Rage back to their table.

Besides Terror, Loco, and Bush, their treasurer, sat Bear and Duke. He was surprised there weren't more of the club there to talk about something as big as the One-Niners.

"Who's watching the bar, Duke?" he asked.

"Jack. She's good. She can handle it for an hour or so." He stared hard at Gunner.

Gunner just grunted and wondered why they had shortened her name to Jack. He wasn't going to ask because it didn't matter to him. Best if he kept his back to the bar and his thoughts to himself.

"Loco managed to reach out to one of our brother clubs where the One-Niners make their home base, in Joplin. Turns out they've pretty much been kicked out by the Holy Terrors. Seems they weren't too thrilled with what the One-Niners were up to." Terror nodded over at Loco.

Loco picked up the conversation. "They've been bad little boys. They started dealing with a terrorist cell that has a training camp up in the hills. Guns and ammo as well as something my contact hasn't discovered yet. Whatever it is, it's the size of a shoebox and comes in plastic tubs of four each. So far they've seen ten of these tubs transferred to the terrorist's compound."

Bush shook his head. "There's no telling what's in those tubs. Could be gun parts for something bigger or parts to make bombs."

"Terrorist tend to lean toward bombs more than anything. Makes the biggest impact with more casualties and collateral damage." Gunner didn't like that some of the bastards had set up shop in their territory. "They've got to go."

"I agree," Rage said. "But we need more information to feed to the Holy Terrors first. I don't want any part of knowing we might have helped to stop an attack if they manage to pull one off."

"I agree." Hawk leaned forward. "Do we know for sure how many are located around Settler's Point?"

"To date we've only spotted three, but that doesn't mean there aren't more on the way or already here and just laying low." Loco nodded toward Bush. "Cowboy and Jinx have been watching them. Right now they're kept to themselves."

"We figure they're waiting on something," Bush said.

"Or someone," Gunner pointed out. "Could be a buy about to go down."

"Not in our town." Terror banged his hand on the table. "Everyone's on alert. We look for anyone who doesn't belong and report back to Loco. He'll keep a log of what we notice and we'll try and map out what they've got in the works. Look for routines and schedules."

"I'll reach out to some of my munition contacts to see if they've been approached by them and if they've delivered anything to them." Gunner started to get up, but Hawk grabbed his arm.

"Wait. There's more."

Gunner slowly returned to his seat and waited. This didn't sound good. They always saved the best for last.

"What do you know about this new girl?" Rage asked him.

"What the fuck?" Gunner sat back in his chair and stared at his president. "As little as I can manage. I haven't spoken more than a half a dozen words with her since we left her ass at the garage the other night."

"Don't you think it's a little too coincidental that she was walking toward town right when we were coming back from our meet up the same time the One-Niners show up?" Terror cocked his head with a serious expression creasing his forehead.

Gunner's first instinct was to defend her, tell them that they were way off base, but he didn't know a thing about her other than she must have some self-hate going on. What if she was with the bastards and had been supposed to infiltrate The Howling Death and feed the other MC information?

"Maybe. It wouldn't be the first time an MC tried that on a rival club," he finally admitted.

Duke groaned. "I'll fire her ass tonight. I can stay and work the bar and let Randy help wait tables. My ass is too big to get between everyone without spilling beer."

"I don't want you to fire her, Duke. We need her where we can watch her." Rage looked back over at Gunner. "I need you to get close to her. Show her some interest, fuck her if you have to, but we need to know if she's a plant."

"Hell no. I'm the last one you want to deal with her. Just looking at her pisses me off," he said.

Rage looked over at Hawk. "You have a problem chatting her up?"

Gunner saw his buddy stiffen up, but he shook his head no. "I can get close to her and feel her out."

"You mean feel her up," Gunner snapped back.

Hawk looked at him. He smiled a toothy smile that was more a look of danger than anything else.

"Gunner, you're with him. Keep his head clear since you don't much like her anyway. He can pump her for information, and you will be there to intervene if things get squirrely." Rage nodded over at his brother. "Anything else?"

Terror nodded. "I want to try and dig into her background. Get me more information as soon as possible, guys."

He and Rage stood. "Be careful, you know the rules. No one goes solo anywhere at any time."

"Hear that, Duke? You can't go potty without me holding your hand," Bear grinned at the other man.

"I'll let you hold something else if you don't fuck off." Duke shot his friend the bird and got up. "I'm out of here. It's been a long day.

"Hold up, man. You can't go without me to make sure you make it home safe." Bear smiled before holding both of his hands up to ward off the other man's attack.

Gunner shook his head. They were steady in a fight and had your back every time, but times like this, their joking around pissed him off. He still couldn't believe Rage expected him to deal with Jackie even knowing how she affected him.

He doesn't know the real reason I don't want to be anywhere around her. I haven't even told Hawk and he's closer to me than my brother by blood.

He just couldn't admit that what had happened with Peggy had left him more scarred than he wanted anyone to know. He had failed her. Left her when she needed him for his brothers in the MC. It didn't matter that he'd tried hard to be there all the time. Only it hadn't been enough even before that night. Gunner knew he had to tell Hawk, but he just couldn't right now. Soon. It had to be real soon.

Chapter Seven

Jackie's feet ached as she finished sweeping the floor. Cindy followed her with the mop, making sure the floor was clean without a sticky layer from spilled beer. The other woman chatted nonstop the entire time they cleaned up. Jackie didn't really mind as long as she didn't expect her to remember anything she said, or to do more than give her an occasional grunt.

"Looks good," Randy told them as he wadded up the bar apron and tossed it in the basket with the dirty rags and towels. "I'll stuff these in the washer and whoever comes in first in the morning can start it. Hold up, and I'll walk you ladies out."

"Where's your car parked, Jack?" Cindy asked her.

"I walked. My truck's over at the garage. Can't get it fixed until I've made enough money for the parts." When the other woman didn't say anything but stopped walking beside her, Jackie turned to look to see what was wrong. "What?"

"You walked? From where?" she asked.

"The motel. It's not that far. The exercise is good for me."

"That's not what she meant, hon." Randy pulled a set of keys out of his pocket. "It's too dangerous to walk around at night. One of us will take you home."

"I will," Cindy said. "The motel is in my direction. You live on the opposite side of town, Randy."

"Look. I'm fine. I've walked in worse places than this. I can take care of myself," she told them, but both stood their ground and shook their heads in solemn agreement.

She refused to say anything more about it. They couldn't make her get into one of their cars if she didn't want to. Once outside, Randy locked the door while Cindy took her hand, urging her to follow her.

"Look. I really appreciate it, but I don't need a ride." She pulled her hand out of the other woman's grip.

Cindy opened her mouth to argue, but the crunch of gravel had her looking up, and her mouth snapped shut.

Expecting it to be Randy behind her intending to make her get into Cindy's car, Jackie turned to snap at him that he wasn't going to manhandle her, only to find that it wasn't the bartender at all. Gunner and Hawk stood behind her with their legs spread wide. Hawk had an easy smile while Gunner's gaze was hot enough it singed her skin.

"Thanks, Cindy. We've got her." Hawk took a step forward. "She's riding with us."

"Oh no I'm not. I don't need anyone to carry me back to the motel. I can get there on my own in one piece. That's more than I can say if I ride with the two of you." Jackie squared her shoulders and stepped away from Cindy and attempted to make a wide path around the two bikers.

"Where do you think you're going, Jack?" Gunner's hand shot out and grabbed her upper arm. His grip was loose, but she knew there'd be no pulling away from it.

As if to make sure of her cooperation, Hawk caged her in from behind. Immediately she felt like the filling in a Hot Pocket. They surrounded her, sealing their warmth in with her until she was sure she felt sweat trickle down her back. The air grew heavy until she was positive she was going to suffocate.

"We're going to give you a ride," Gunner told her with a growl in his voice. "Tonight and every night that you work."

"Why? What's changed? One minute you can't stand for me to be in the same town and now you expect me to believe you care what happens to me? Well screw you, Gunner." Jackie tried to push past the big biker, but he stood his ground wearing a predatory grin.

"Gunner was fighting his attraction to you, but I convinced him there was no use. He's relationship shy, but I'm not. Can't really call it a relationship when you're just passing through, now can I." Hawk's warm breath puffed along her ear even as that dirty, deep voice plucked at the strings controlling her hormones.

Holy hell!

It took a full thirty seconds for her to remember how to form a coherent word, much less a complete sentence. She searched her memory until the one that contradicted Hawk's statement jumped out in her mind.

"That's bullcrap. He took one look at the scars on my wrist and snarled at me like I was a leper. I highly doubt he's changed his mind," she said.

If that had startled Hawk, he didn't show it. Evidently he'd already known about the scars. They didn't step away from her either.

"We need to get you back to the motel and talk this over in a more private location," Hawk said instead.

"There's nothing to discuss. Leave me the fuck alone. I don't need your kind of trouble." Again Jackie tried to push between them but to no avail.

"Stop fighting us, Jackie. We aren't bringing you any trouble," Gunner said. He sighed. "We want to start over. Can't you give us another chance?"

"You didn't have a chance to begin with. I don't have time for hookups or even quickies against that wall over there, so stuff it and move out of my way." Jackie was beginning to panic. She could fight with the best of them, but there were two of them, and they weren't your average punk intent on robbery or even rape.

Faster than a hawk diving on its prey, Gunner had her over his shoulder, following Hawk as they walked across the back lot to where two bikes were parked side by side. The move had been so quick and smooth as silk that Jackie was still trying to regain her focus when they stopped next to the bikes.

"What are you doing?" she yelled.

"Hold her while I get on," Gunner told the other man then transferred her to Hawk's arms.

"Hey! I'm talking to you, asshole."

"What does it look like I'm doing?" Gunner threw one leg over the bike, straddling it before he started the impressive engine. "Okay, Hawk."

Her ride lifted her over the back of the bike before shoving Gunner's helmet on her head. As soon as Hawk stepped away from the revving motor of the iron horse she found herself riding, Gunner took off. Jackie let out a high-pitched squeal as she wrapped her arms around Gunner's impressive six-pack and held on for dear life. She swore as they pulled out of the bar's parking lot that she heard Hawk laugh.

* * * *

Hawk watched Jackie scramble to wrap her arms around Gunner as his friend lurched forward across the lot at a face clip. The woman's shriek of surprise made it so that he couldn't help but laugh. That had been all woman. Despite her tough-as-nails attitude, there was still a feminine streak inside her. It might be buried deep, but it was still there.

Frankly, he liked her just like she was. In an MC's world, there wasn't a lot of room for wimps or girly girls. Mia was an exception. She was Terror and Rage's old lady. Despite her sweet but shy demeanor, the woman was as solid as they came. She'd gone through hell while on the run from her deceased husband's boss. Now she was happy with the two bikers and supported them wholeheartedly.

He wanted to talk to his friend about her, but without his helmet on, Gunner didn't have access to the radio. If they had longer than a short minute's ride to the motel, Hawk would have talked dirty to her over the radio in the helmet. But they were already pulling into the lot.

Gunner turned back and yelled something at Jackie. She pointed toward the back, so he and Gunner drove around the building until she pointed to a particular door. Hawk parked the bike and jumped off to help Jackie down from behind Gunner.

"That wasn't so bad, now was it?" Hawk removed the helmet and smiled at the picture she made with the way the static electricity formed a small mountain on top of her head.

Once Gunner had climbed off the bike, Hawk tried to smooth Jackie's hair down, but she slapped his hands away and did it herself. He couldn't help but chuckle at the sight. Her hair had already been a slight mess from working first in a hot, greasy kitchen then out on the floor waiting tables in a mad rush to keep everyone in beer. Now she'd just had a quick ride wearing a helmet too large for her head. There was no wonder her hair looked a mess.

"Thanks for the ride. You can go now." She turned her back on them as she pulled the key from her pocket and inserted it into the lock.

"We still need to talk, princess," Hawk told her.

"There's nothing to talk about. I'm not interested. Period." She shoved her door open, stepping in. She'd tried to close it even before she'd turned around but Gunner had one booted foot lodged in the doorway.

"Oh, we've got plenty to talk about, babe. First of all, we need to discuss your sassy mouth and attitude. While it turns me on something fierce, it also pisses me off when I'm serious," Gunner said. "Move back so you don't get hurt."

Hawk could see the wheels turning in her head as she weighed her options. For a brief second, she looked as if she were going to argue and fight them, but logic won out and instead of trying to shove the door closed again, Jackie stepped back and walked across the small room to take a seat in the only available chair.

He could easily imagine by her small smile that she'd chalked a win up to her by claiming the chair for herself. Gunner, for all his bravado that he was just there to be sure Hawk didn't fall for anything she tried to lay on him, took the lead and stalked across the room to stand over her. It amused Hawk to no end. He just walked over to the bedside table across from them and made his own place to sit.

"This is how it's going to be," Gunner began. "As long as you're in town, you're ours. Got it?"

Before he could continue, Jackie growled and stood to poke Gunner in the chest with a single finger while she seethed out her argument.

"I don't belong to anyone. Do you hear me? No. One. Except me. You don't get to treat me like a leper then claim me like I'm a pet. Take your stupid ultimatums and fuck off. Right out that door there." Jackie pointed toward the now-closed and locked door.

Hawk got a slight glimpse of the scars she'd mentioned earlier. He'd covered his surprise and sudden understanding then, but now it hit him again just what his friend's beef was with the pretty woman really was. Hell, he couldn't even blame him. Why would someone want to kill themselves? Why? If you don't like your situation, you move on.

He caught her looking at him, obviously realizing he was staring at the scar he could see. She didn't lower her eyes, just glared before looking back up to the man in front of her.

"Get. The. Fuck. Out. Now! You want to pay my repair bill? Fine. Give me an address where I can mail your money to you, and I'll accept it." She propped her hands on her hips and waited.

Hawk hadn't realized his club brother had offered. No wonder he'd been pissed off since he'd talked to her at the bar. He waited to see what Gunner would say. If he got her out of town, it would end any speculation of her being a plant for the One-Niners. There was no way she would take that offer if she was supposed to spy on them.

"No." Gunner cocked his head with a wide, dangerous-looking smile. "You should have taken that offer before I gave in. There's no way I'm letting you get away until I've had my fill of you now, Jack."

The woman's face paled, and she started to take a step back but the back of her legs hit the chair, and she sat down hard. For a split second, Hawk wondered if she'd pass out. Was she actually as terrified of them as it appeared? Then her expression changed. Her mouth drooped, and her eyes shuttered as she stared down at her hands resting on her knees.

"I'm not interested in any kind of relationship with you. Not a short term, not a hookup for sex, or anything else. I'm just not interested. I don't think you are either. So what is that you want from me?"

Hawk slid off the table and walked over to kneel next to the chair. "Honey, we just want some time with you to get to know you. Things didn't start out on the right foot before, but that's because you shocked Gunner, here."

He felt Gunner stiffen then heard him release a harsh breath. He knelt in front of her, as well. Hawk could feel the turmoil in his friend and hated that they had to do this. It wasn't fair to Gunner or even to the woman, especially if she didn't have any part of the issue with the One-Niners.

"Look. I had a woman years ago who committed suicide. I didn't understand then, and I still don't understand now why. I did everything I knew to do to make her happy, but it wasn't enough. If she wasn't happy, why didn't she just leave? Why did she have to do that?" He shook his head and looked up at her. "Why did you?"

A slow, full minute passed in complete silence. Finally, she sighed and pulled the numerous bracelets and support bands off. The scars on both wrists were numerous and thick. To Hawk, it looked as if she'd tried more than a couple of times to end it all. That didn't sit well with him either. He had to swallow back the bile that rushed up his throat.

"You don't know anything about me or my past. You just make assumptions and treat me based on those assumptions. Do you really care why? Does it matter that much?" she asked in a quiet voice.

Gunner stood and paced. Hawk didn't move. He wanted to know why, but Gunner was fighting that need. Knowing more about her past and those scars would make her more than a job to them, and he knew it. Not knowing would eat him up inside.

Finally, he stopped pacing, stopping in front of her. He didn't bend down to answer her. Instead, he stood there for a few seconds staring up at the ceiling. When he looked over at Hawk, he could see the pain and resignation in his friend's eyes.

"Yeah. I want to know why. What was so horrible that you didn't think you could do anything except put an end to your life? Tell us."

Chapter Eight

Jackie swallowed around the knot in her throat. She'd hoped he would say no, he didn't give a damn what her reasons were. Instead, he'd said yes, and she wasn't prepared to bare her life's sins to them. They were bikers, they'd probably killed before. Nothing should shock them.

And nothing will seem terrible enough to warrant what they believed about me. To them, life is crap and you made it yours.

They didn't know that nothing had been hers in a long time. Now, she was all she had.

Jackie closed her eyes and started talking. If she didn't see their faces while she gave them what they wanted, maybe it wouldn't be as hard. Maybe.

"I'm not going to bore you with the details of what life was like as a kid. My father was a worthless drunk. Mom nearly worked herself to death to keep food on the table. That left us with him all day and sometimes later at night. He was abusive and loud. One day he went on a shooting spree and killed everyone but me. I didn't escape unharmed, but I survived when no one else did. Not even him." She shifted on the chair.

"Fast forward past the hospital, the foster homes, and the struggle to get through school while I worked. When I turned nineteen, I had two years of community college behind me. I'd managed to graduate high school early and aged out of the system, so I was on my own. I applied to several colleges close by but only qualified for partial scholarships. I couldn't work and make enough money to live and pay the balance of my education, so I decided to try again later."

Jackie drew in a soft breath, trying to force herself to relax again so that she could get through this. Baring her life to someone she didn't know was harder than she'd thought it would be. Once she'd paid for her truck's repairs, she would leave this place and never see these men again. It shouldn't be this hard.

"One of the men on the scholarship committee offered to pay the balance for me, and I could pay him back once I had settled into a good job after graduation. I couldn't believe that my luck was finally turning around. I believed it was my time and never once worried that I was making a mistake.

"The first few months of college were exciting for me. I loved learning and enjoyed the interaction with the other teenagers and young adults I made friends with. I'd never had a friend before. With my father, it had been impossible. Foster homes meant the only people who would come around you were the kids you lived with and the many social workers. Parents wouldn't allow their children to play with us or even befriend us. We were the lowest of society's dregs. To them, we came from drug homes and worthless parents. It didn't matter that some of the kids had lost their parents in accidents and had lived in nice homes until then."

"You say that like it didn't matter how they treated you, it was the ones who'd had good homes that mattered." She felt Hawk's hand brush her hair back from her face.

"I mattered, but it was wrong that they lumped us all together without giving anyone a chance. One of the kids I met in one of the homes had lived in a mansion before his parents were killed in a plane crash. He didn't have any other family alive to take him. His inheritance was placed in a trust for when he got out, but he didn't make it out." She swallowed back the tears for the poor little boy he'd been.

"What happened?" It was Gunner who asked this time.

"The home we were living in at the time was in a bad part of the city. We couldn't go anywhere alone. There were gangs and pimps and all sorts of people there. One morning we were standing at the bus stop to go to school, and a car drove by spraying bullets all over the area. Two of my fellow foster kids were killed, and one ended up in a wheelchair for the rest of her life."

"What about you?" Hawk asked.

"I only had a couple of cuts where the bullets shaved my arm and my hip. I was treated and released back into the same foster home."

Nothing was said for a few minutes as Jackie readjusted her position on the chair. There was one spring that poked her left hip a little bit. She'd forgotten and hadn't paid attention how she'd sat after giving Gunner a piece of her mind. Now she was paying for it.

"Nothing changed? You still walked to the same bus stop and waited for the school bus?" Hawk asked her.

"Oh things changed. They moved three new kids in two days later. We stayed until the husband got sick and the woman had to take care of him instead of us. Honestly, we could have stayed. She never did anything. We cooked and cleaned and took care of the younger ones. But the system didn't allow it."

"Why didn't you tell the social workers that you were running the house by yourself anyway? That should have woken them up to move you out." Gunner's voice sounded off to her. She wasn't sure why, but she refused to look at him. If she did, Jackie was sure she'd lose the ability to continue.

"We weren't about to complain about a little work that made life easier for us. Most of us had been in really horrible homes in the past and didn't want to end up in another one. It was safer to keep our mouths shut."

"That's all kinds of wrong. You know that, don't you?" Gunner asked.

Jackie just shrugged. "It is what it is. We survived. At least everyone did while were in the same foster homes. I counted that as a win."

"Get her something to drink, Gunner." Hawk moved until he sat right in front of her and scrubbed his hands over his face.

"Here." Gunner had opened one of her Diet Cokes and shoved it in her hands.

It tasted wonderful and was cold going down. She hadn't realized how dry her mouth had been. She did notice how tired she was, though. A quick look over at the clock on the table next to the bed told her it was after three in the morning.

"Anyway, to make all of this shorter, I ended up moving in to the apartment over the garage at this man's house when someone broke into my little apartment one night while I was there. He insisted that I needed to find a safer place. I couldn't find anything I could afford, so he told me I could live in the apartment he had. I didn't see anything wrong with it. He hadn't tried to move me in right away after he offered to pay for the balance of my college tuition.

"When the first year had ended, I'd planned to continue on in summer school, but he talked me into working instead and not pushing myself by trying to finish all at once. I should have realized then that something was up, but it made sense to me then, too. So I found a second job and started saving money to pay him back and have a little nest egg for when I graduated. I thought my life was going to be different now. I'd be able to get a good job after school and eventually have a normal relationship with people. But that changed when I got off late one night and started to unlock the door to the little apartment. He caught me by surprise, so I never saw his hand when it covered my mouth and nose with the cloth covered in ether. I woke up in what I later learned was his basement in a five-by-five-foot cage."

* * * *

Gunner stared at the woman. What the hell? That only happened in third world countries or in books and horror pictures. Did she really think they'd believe her? He started to say as much, but Hawk knew what he was thinking and stopped him with a squeeze to his shoulder. The other man had gotten up and was leaning against the wall next to him now.

"What happened when you woke up, Jackie?" Hawk asked.

The fact that she still wouldn't look at them grated on Gunner's nerves. He figured she was hiding the fact that she was spinning them a tale. He was sure it would be obvious if he could see her eyes.

"I was violently ill off and on for several hours. I found out later that he'd put the bucket in there because he knew that. He'd done this several times before. I hadn't been the first one who'd fallen for the tricks hidden by an altruistic mask. I was just the one who put an end to it." She hesitated then continued. "Three years later."

"He kept you in his basement for three fucking years?" Hawk pushed off the wall with one booted foot and walked the width of the room back and forth for several minutes before he returned to sit on the floor in front of her. "Why? What did he want with you?"

Gunner was stunned that Hawk was falling for her story. He started to leave, but something about the way she cleared her throat and shrugged made him stay. He sat on the edge of the bed and waited to hear what she'd say.

"I don't know. I mean he." She stuttered for a second. "Did things to me and hurt me, but I don't know what he got out of it. He didn't physically rape me or anything. He didn't even jack off after he'd finished with me for the night. I can't even imagine what he got out of it, but I honestly didn't care. I just wanted out. The pain and constant uncertainty about what was coming next was too much for me to deal with."

"How did you survive that? What did you do?" Hawk asked her, taking her hands into his before looking over at Gunner.

He could see the compassion and maybe even a little censure for him in his friend's eyes. It didn't change how he felt, that she was making it all up, but it hurt him all the same.

"I didn't have much of a choice. One day, I don't know how long I had been down there, he made the mistake of leaving a glass on the floor near my cage. When he had finished with me, he shoved me in and locked it but forgot the glass. I lay there for hours just trying to get past the pain. I looked at that glass the entire time, knowing he'd finally given me a chance to escape.

"It took several tries to reach it. I could get my hand through the bars, but my arm would only go so far through the bars before there just wasn't room anymore. I worked on pushing my skin through a little at a time until my arm moved a tiny fraction of an inch. Finally I could touch the glass with my fingertips. I was afraid I would tip it over the wrong way, so I worked more of my arm through the bars until I could get the tip of one finger over the edge and pull it over in my direction."

"Is that when it broke?" Gunner asked, uncaring that a little sarcasm seeping into his voice.

"No. It didn't break. I rolled it over toward me and had to work my arm back through the bars again so I could slide it down closer to the ground. Then I picked it up and smashed it against the concrete floor. A piece of it cut the palm of my hand, but really, why did that matter when I was going to cut my wrists anyway." She sighed before taking a drink from the can then shoving it between her legs again.

Before Hawk could take her hands in his again, Gunner walked over and grabbed her hands to turn them over. Sure enough, there was a scar on the palm of her right hand.

So what? I still don't believe she isn't making this up. She could have done that herself without all the bullshit story she's feeding us.

It caught him by surprise when she jerked her hand from his and buried both of hers under her thighs. She brought her head up for a quick second before she continued looking down again. In that minute second, he'd seen unfathomable pain and anger there. It had been so raw that Gunner wasn't sure what to believe anymore. Was she telling the truth?

"I grabbed the largest piece I could and wrapped one end in a piece of the sheet he'd given me to sleep under. Since he kept me naked, I didn't have anything on me to use. I knew if I didn't have a safe end to hold on to, I wouldn't be able to cut deep enough because of the pain. It took two tries for me to actually do it. After I got past the first cut, I sliced through it again then did the same to the other one. It was harder to do. Not because I was worried about the pain anymore. It was because that hand was weak and didn't work right after I'd cut it.

"I thought about cutting my neck, but I wasn't really sure where to cut, and both of my hands were weak now. I just lay back and prayed God wouldn't disown me because of what I had done. I confessed my sins, told him I was sorry for being so weak, and a few minutes later, I passed out."

Gunner realized he'd matched his breathing to hers that was coming in quick breaths as if she were reliving that moment in time. He steadied his then rubbed one hand over his eyes. There was no emotion in her voice, but he had plenty for both of them. Somewhere in all of that, he'd started believing that at least some of it were true.

"What happened that you didn't bleed out and die?" Hawk asked after a few seconds of quiet.

"He decided to check on me that morning before he left for school. Sometimes he did, but usually he didn't. He only fed me once a day, so normally I was left alone except for three or four hours each evening after he'd come home and had eaten. This time he found me still alive and sewed up my wrists. I'm glad I wasn't conscious to have to go through that as well as the anger I'm sure he'd had over what I'd done." She rolled her shoulders, pulling her hands from beneath her to take a drink from the can again.

"He didn't take you to an emergency room?" Hawk cursed under his breath. "I guess he couldn't without you telling someone what was happening to you. Son of a bitch."

"He probably figured if I lived through it that was good enough. If I didn't, he'd bury me out back like he had the other women. I remember rousing briefly as he poured water and something like Gatorade into me. Then I was out until sometime later.

"My wrists were bandaged and tied to either side of the cage so I couldn't dig out the stitches I guess. The thought had crossed my mind. I didn't have much energy anyway. One of my arms had just enough slack in it that I could reach the open jug of water he'd left and the plastic bowl of cheese and bread. I ate and drank because I didn't know what else to do. He'd taken my one chance away from me. I think I lost all hope then." She looked up again, giving them both a glimpse of what she must have felt during that time. Utter and complete hopelessness. Gunner could see an emptiness there that was a little scary.

"I spent more and more time in my own head. It kept me from being aware of what was happening to me for the most part. Sometimes he'd realize what I was doing and jerk me back so that I couldn't escape the pain and humiliation. I guess he finally wasn't getting what he wanted or needed out of me and decided it was time to move on to a new woman."

"What did he do? I know he wasn't about to let you free to report him. You said he'd buried the other girls in the back yard. How did you know that? Did he tell you about them?" Gunner still couldn't believe all of her story, but more and more of it seemed real to him now.

"Don't bombard her with questions, man. Let her get this out her way. I can't imagine that it's easy to reveal something like this to strangers." Hawk stared at him, but this time he seemed almost beaten.

Gunner realized that his friend was living this with her to the extent that someone could. He'd bought into the entire story and was empathizing with her to a degree that it affected his expressions and the way his eyes shown bright when he looked at Gunner.

"Go on, Jackie. What happened?"

"One night he carried a small plastic basin down when he got home. I knew it was earlier than usual and figured he'd skipped his meal for the night. He pulled me out of the cage and strapped me down to one of the odd-shaped tables he had down there. Then he washed and braided my hair. I almost smiled. I knew from the past that when he braided my hair, he planned to kill me. It was finally over, so I didn't care what else he did to me. I mean, washing and braiding my hair didn't faze me.

"My arms were strapped to the table, but my wrists and hands were free. While he bent over me, my hand brushed against the knife he carried in his belt. I couldn't believe my luck. The next time he bumped against me I slipped it out and shoved it under my hip, praying it wouldn't show and he wouldn't notice that it was missing. He'd finished what he had planned to do and left me there. I figured he'd gone to dig my grave next to the others.

"Being alone didn't bother me. I equated being alone to being without pain. It was a welcome part of my life at that point. The weaker I got, the more I didn't want to die. I don't know what was different compared to the time I'd tried to kill myself unless it was because he was the one to kill me and I didn't want him to have that privilege. It hadn't been my choice to end my life. It had been his, and I wasn't going to let him win." She drew in a deep breath and lifted her head to stare at them.

Gunner almost took a step back at the amount of rage and determination on her face. A bright light shined from her eyes that was more like madness than anything else. It spooked him. He couldn't imagine what she had described and still wasn't sure how much of it he could believe. The one thing he did believe in that moment was what he saw in her eyes, a fierceness that could only be described as bravery in the face of certain death.

"I struggled against the straps, but they were too tight for me to try and slip out. I worked the knife out from under me and started trying to cut the straps holding me down. I had to focus on making my fingers work to locate the handle of the knife. I managed to cut my fingers before I found the handle, but I managed to cut one free then the other.

"I panted trying to slow my breathing so that I didn't pass out by hyperventilating. My hand and fingers were bleeding from all the botched attempts at getting free. I knew holding my arms up would slow the amount that came out, but I couldn't hold them up forever."

"It had to have taken a lot of determination to do it," Hawk told her. "Not only because of your hands being cut but also because of what all you had already been through. That's amazing."

She shrugged. "No. Maybe if I hadn't already tried to kill myself, it would have been."

"If you had been meant to die, you would have," Gunner finally spoke up.

"Maybe." Jackie sighed. "After I managed to get free, I wasn't sure what to do next. I was sure I was locked in, and if I wasn't, he'd see me trying to get away. I didn't think I had a lot of time. I decided to wait at the top of the stairs and see if I could hear anything. If he was up and moving around, I hoped I'd hear it and know to wait. At the last minute, I grabbed the knife to carry with me.

"There were exactly twelve steps up to the door. I counted them as I climbed up. I nearly fell twice. I was so tired, and I couldn't seem to catch my breath. When I reached the top one, I sat down and pressed my ear to the door. I couldn't hear anything at all. I wasn't sure if he was asleep in bed, on a chair, or if I just couldn't hear anything. It felt as if every minute lasted an hour. And with each one that passed, I seemed sleepier and sleepier. I had to remind myself to breathe. It made me angry that I had gotten this far and might fail. I guess the anger gave me enough strength to keep going."

Gunner watched her as she rubbed at the scars on her wrists. First one then the other, and she repeated it over and over until Hawk grabbed her hands to stop her. He was glad someone had sense in that moment. He was completely helpless. Her words were far too real now. She had described exactly what it had felt like the time he'd been shot and nearly bled out before Hawk had gotten to him.

"What did you do, Jackie?" Hawk finally asked her.

"I managed to get to my feet, and I checked to see if the doorknob would turn. If it didn't, I was going to try and force the slide out of the door. Wasn't much of a plan, but I wasn't giving up. The knob turned, though, and I found myself in his kitchen. I couldn't believe it. I was going to make it. Before I reached the back door, though, he walked in with a shocked expression. I think we stared at each other for an entire minute before he yelled at me and started toward me. I groped for the knob on the back door and tried to open it, but it would budge. I realized later that there was a deadbolt I had to throw first.

"When he snagged my braid and tried to pull me backward, I slashed at him with the knife I still had in one hand. It hit his forearm, and the impact jarred my wrists to the bone. He screamed, and then I can't really remember what happened after that. I just know that we fought and he ended up on top of me with the knife in his chest, dead."

Chapter Nine

Jackie sat there without saying anything else for a long time. It felt as if she'd run a marathon. She was sweating, exhausted, and panting like a dog. Just going back over it had drained her. At least she hadn't thrown up this time.

"Are you okay, Jackie?" Hawk asked, gently squeezing her hands in his.

"Yeah. I'm good. After I finally rolled him off of me and realized he was dead, I crawled over to the phone on the counter and managed to grab it. I dialed 911 and just started crying. The police and ambulance showed up and took me to the hospital. I spent four days there before I was released. The cops asked a lot of questions, but I guess my injuries and the basement pretty much told the story."

Jackie sighed and picked up the can for another drink, but it was empty. Gunner walked over to the little fridge and pulled another one out. After he'd opened it, he helped her hold it until her hands quit shaking. It tasted so good. She savored the slight burn as it went down. The first few swallows of a soda were always the best.

"Anyway, they told me later that they'd uncovered four other female bodies in his back yard and all of their personal items had been locked in his safe. They returned mine to me later. One of the cops was an older man. He brought his wife to help me dress and get ready to be discharged. He seemed to know that I wasn't going to trust anyone again. He was right. It was a long time before I could stand to be in the same room with a man.

"They told me that the only reason I had survived to call the police was because the cuts in my hand and fingers were shallow and would have taken a good deal of time for me to bleed out. At that point, I didn't care. Instead, I had to figure out how to survive in a world that I no longer felt safe in. I had to find somewhere to live and a job to pay for it. Oddly enough, the court awarded me with a couple thousand dollars from his estate to reestablish myself. I'm not sure I would have made it without that."

Jackie watched as Hawk slowly stood and held out his hand to her. Gunner walked over and held out his hand, as well. Jackie took another swallow of her Diet Coke then Gunner took it from her. She let them pull her to her feet and guide her over to the bed.

"Let's get you ready for bed. I didn't realize how late it had gotten. You must be exhausted." Hawk urged her to sit then knelt to remove her boots and socks. "Fuck!"

"What?" Gunner dropped to his knees next to him. "What is it?"

"Look at the blisters on her feet. I told you those boots weren't good for walking." Hawk shook his head. "Can't do anything about it now. I'll get some salve and bring it by after lunch, hon."

"Don't worry about it. I'm planning to go by and get some better shoes when I get up in the morning." She looked over at the clock and groaned. "Later this morning."

"No you're not, babe. You're staying in bed till at least noon. We'll get you some salve and a pair of house shoes to wear to the store to pick out something better for your feet. I'll tell Scoot and Duke that you won't be working until those blisters heal." Gunner sighed and ran his hands through his hair. She noticed again how there appeared to be silver or gray highlights in his brown hair that poked up after he'd plowed his fingers through it.

When she looked over at Hawk, she couldn't help but admire the way his darker brown hair curled a little as it almost brushed the tip of his shoulders. She had the urge to run her hands through it to see if it was as soft as it looked. Unlike Gunner, there wasn't a scar visible on his face, but his hazel eyes appeared older than his real age. For a second, she wondered if she was older than either of the men.

"Let's get your clothes off and you into bed." Hawk stood after setting her boots and socks to the side.

"I can handle getting undressed, Hawk. I don't need anyone's help with that." Jackie didn't want to see the pity on their faces if they saw her body with all the scars.

"Gunner, get her a warm bath cloth to wash her face," Hawk continued as if she hadn't said a word.

She didn't bother fighting him when he pulled off her shirt. He was stronger than she was and she guessed it really didn't matter one way or another what they saw. She wasn't going to be there more than a month or two at the most.

"Mother fuck!" Gunner's voice behind her made her hang her head for a second. Then she turned and looked at him over her shoulder.

"Don't stare at me. Give me the damn cloth." She held out one hand and curled her fingers.

He looked up to meet her gaze then walked around the bed to hand her the warm, wet cloth. She washed her face then her neck before handing it back to him expecting that he'd return it to the bathroom. Instead, he tossed it in that direction and continued to stand there while Hawk made her lie back so he could remove her jeans.

"I don't want you standing on those blisters unless you have to. Let us take care of this." Hawk nodded at Gunner, and they each took a leg and pulled down after she'd unfastened them and shoved them as far down her hips as she could manage.

"There you go. Get some sleep, Jackie," Hawk said.

"Don't get out of this bed until we knock on the door to bring you the salve and shoes. I mean it, babe. We kept you up all night nosing where we had no business. I'm sorry." Gunner turned and strode to the door where he kept his back to her while he waited on Hawk to join him.

When they'd closed it behind them, and the automatic lock clicked into place, Jackie relaxed against the mattress and closed her eyes. She couldn't believe she wasn't crying, but somehow it had been good for her to talk about it out loud. She realized it had been cathartic to tell them about it. There'd been more, but it was only a blip in her history. Not worth thinking about really. It had been bad luck and nothing more.

The last thing she thought about before she drifted off was that she hoped this wasn't going to end up being another bad memory in a long trail of dark ones she ended up locking away. She was kind of tired of all the bad luck and wanted something to be normal for a change.

* * * *

Jackie jerked awake at the pounding on the door. She scrubbed at her eyes trying to remember where she was and why someone was beating on her door. Then she remembered and managed to focus on the clock on the bedside table. Twelve thirty. From the light seeping into the room around the blackout drapes, it was daytime.

"Fuck!"

She needed more sleep, but she had to be at work at six anyway. She still needed shoes and something to eat, not necessarily in that order. Crap. Who was beating on the fucking door?

Jackie cringed as she dropped her sore feet to the floor and stood. It didn't get any easier when she walked across the floor to the door either. She slipped the drapes to one side and groaned.

Gunner.

She opened the door and let him in. Short of causing a scene, Jackie figured that was the only way to settle the matter.

"Come on, babe. Back to bed and off those feet. I've got some medicine and a pair of house shoes that should work for now. We'll go get some decent shoes for you later."

"Thanks for the medicine. I'll put it on after I get dressed. I've got a lot to do before I go in to work tonight."

"You're not going on those feet, Jackie." Gunner's deep voice didn't carry the soothing quality that Hawk's did.

"I'm going to work. If you ruin this for me, I'll find another way to get out of this town without the money."

"Fuck, Jack. Fine. First, let's tend to your feet then we'll go get something to eat. You're bound to be starving."

She sat up against the headboard and crossed one leg so that she could check out the messy blisters on one foot. They weren't going to be comfortable to stand on even with the best of shoes. She'd need a soft innersole to cushion them.

Gunner strode across the floor to the bathroom then returned a couple of minutes later with a warm, wet bath cloth. He gently pressed the cloth to the bottoms of her feet until he felt they were clean enough to bandage. She growled at him when he applied some sort of salve that stung a little.

"I thought you were supposed to be making them feel better, not burn me."

"The salve will heal the blisters faster than just applying an antibiotic salve and slapping a bandage over them."

"I'm not convinced."

He chuckled. "That's because it still hurts a little. They'll feel better in a few hours. It's going to take several days to heal them so that they don't hurt some when you walk on them. Especially if you insist on going back to work."

"I can handle the pain." She waited while he applied the bandages. "I need the work. I have to eat and pay the rent on this place, so not working isn't an option."

"Once Hawk gets here we'll go get something to eat then see about some shoes. See if you can stand up now."

Jackie slid over to the edge of the bed and gently stood on her newly bandaged feet. They burned, but they weren't quite as tender as before. She pulled her clothes out of her suitcase, thankful to have all her things from the truck now.

"I'm going to get dressed. I'll be out in a few minutes." She left Gunner sitting on the bed as she closed the bathroom door behind her.

What in the hell am I going to do with them? I was hoping last night was just some sort of bad dream. Now it looks like I have a pair of bikers intent on being my escorts for the day.

"Wonderful."

She brushed her teeth, washed her face, and finished her toiletries before pulling on a fresh pair of jeans and a T-shirt. She fooled with her hair then pulled it back in a ponytail to keep it out of her eyes. The sound of a bike pulling up outside the motel told her that her time was up, and she needed to face them. If she were lucky, they would agree to leave her alone. She'd pressure them after she had something to eat. Gunner was right, she was starved.

The motel door opened then closed again before she walked out of the bathroom. Hawk and Gunner stood by the door talking. Hawk looked up and gave her a biker version of a smile most people would call smartass.

"How are you feeling today?" Hawk asked.

"I'm good. Feet feel better, but the house shoes help that."

"Let's ride, doll. I'm hungry, so I'm sure you are, as well."

"Can't say that I've ever ridden on back of a bike with house shoes before." She stepped out of the room behind Hawk with Gunner closing the door behind them.

Hawk chuckled. "First for me, too. Hold on and keep your shoes on the spikes. Don't know how the shoes will hold up if you hit one of the pipes, so don't do it."

Jackie had no plans of getting her feet burned on top of the killer blisters. She'd make double sure her feet were where they were supposed to be.

Gunner helped her climb on the back of Hawk's bike then the two bikes roared out of the parking lot of the motel. Jackie cringed. She sure hoped the old woman was slightly deaf or she was going to lose her temporary home.

The quick trip to the diner took all of sixty seconds. It took longer for her to climb down off the bike and give Hawk his helmet back than it had to get there. She followed Gunner inside with Hawk trailing this time. They seemed intent on keeping her between them, which should have bothered her, but for some reason, it made her feel protected.

The waitress wasn't the same one she'd met the day before. This one had mid length blonde hair that obviously came out of a bottle since her darker roots needed some cover up. She crossed the room in a slow stride meant to give them time to get seated before she asked for their drink order. Hawk held her chair at the dingy Formica table. Jackie felt awkward as she sat, unused to that type of treatment.

"What can I get ya' to drink, guys?"

"We want tea," Gunner said. "What about you, babe?"

"Um, water's fine."

"Need menus?" the waitress asked, holding them out."

"She will. We don't." Hawk snagged one of the menus and handed it to her.

"Their food is pretty good here. Nothing like bar's crap," Gunner said.

"What are you guys getting?" She was sure they'd know what was best on the menu so she'd probably get whatever they wanted.

"Meatloaf and mashed potatoes." Hawk pointed it out on the menu she held in her hand.

"Sounds good to me. I'll get the same thing."

When the waitress returned with their drinks, Hawk gave her their order. She nodded and walked over to the counter where she called it out to the cook in the back.

"The only real store here in town that might have what you want for your feet is the general store. There are a few specialty shops that have shoes, but mostly they're fancy heels and not what I assume you're going to need for standing on your feet at night." Gunner added a little sugar to his tea and stirred it.

"I just want a good pair of tennis shoes, or if they have some work shoes, I'll get them. I'll pad them with an innersole, and that should work fine." She sipped at her water.

"Where are you from? Generally speaking, of course," Hawk asked her.

"Tennessee. Traveled around some, but mostly in TN."

"They get drive-bys over there?" Gunner stirred his tea with his knife.

"They do in Memphis. That's where I ended up when my dad shot everyone. We lived in a little nothing town just outside the Memphis city limits."

"I'd heard Memphis was a little Chicago," Hawk said.

"Gangs are tough there. They rule the streets, and even the cops don't like messing in their territories."

"Where are you headed to?"

"Not sure yet. I want to drive up to Farmington, Missouri and see if an aunt I used to know still lives there or not. Haven't seen her in about twenty years. My dad ran her off when she'd come visit so my mom told her not to come back so there wouldn't be any trouble."

They talked about the weather, the bar and then their meal arrived and talk stopped. The meatloaf was excellent, and the mashed potatoes were like the ones her mom had made when she was a kid, complete with small lumps and a creamy texture surrounding them. She scarfed up the food as if she hadn't eaten in days instead of hours. It would tide her through until she got a short break to eat at the bar later that night.

"That was delicious. You were right about the meatloaf." She drained her glass and waited on the waitress to bring their checks.

"Dessert, guys?" the blonde asked.

"Not today. What about you, Jackie?" Hawk moved his plate to one side and set his elbows on the table. "There's plenty of time if you want some."

"No thanks. I'm stuffed."

"Just the ticket then, Gail."

She tore the paper off her pad and handed it to Hawk. Jackie held out her hand but was met with a frown from Gail.

"It's all together, doll. We're paying for your meal."

"I pay for my own meals." She had to grit her teeth to keep from raising her voice.

"Not when you're with us, you don't." Gunner winked at her. "You belong to us, so we pay."

"What did I tell you yesterday?"

"Not here, babe. We'll settle this back at the hotel after we've gotten your shoes." Gunner got up and reached for her hand.

She refused the hand and got up on her own. Then gingerly walked ahead of both men to the door. They could pay and catch up later. She was pissed off that they were carrying the entire *ours* issue too far.

She knew she couldn't walk anywhere with her feet as tender as they were, or she'd have headed out toward Main Street by herself. Instead, she stood with crossed arms next to Hawk's bike and waited.

The ride to Settler's Point General Store took about as long as it had taken to get to the diner from the hotel. She figured they could ride the entire town in less than fifteen minutes if they obeyed the speed limits. The place spread out but wasn't really all that large.

She browsed through the shoes and found a pair that would fit with the innersoles to cushion her feet. She put both pair on and walked around for a few minutes before deciding that they'd do. She paid for them and had the cashier put her borrowed house shoes in the box to give back to Gunner. When they found her standing near the front of the store, a scowl converted their faces into less than happy expressions.

"You've already bought the shoes." Gunner seemed to be accusing her of something.

"Well, yeah. That's what I came for, and I found what I needed so I checked out. I didn't know how long it would take for you guys to get whatever you were looking for."

Hawk slammed his hands on his hips and looked at the ceiling as if looking for an answer of some kind there. Then he shook his head and stared at her.

"We were going to get the shoes for you since you need them for work. Are you sure you got what you wanted? Hell, it normally takes a woman at least an hour of shopping to find what she wants."

"I'm not most women. I don't like shopping. I just find what I need and leave. These are good shoes, so there's no reason to mess around." Jackie held up one shoe for their inspection. "See. They fit, and they don't hurt my feet. I can feel the blisters, but they won't get worse in these shoes."

"Fine. Let's go." Hawk didn't argue anymore.

She had a feeling that wasn't going to be the end of their conversation when they got back to the motel. She still needed to make sure they understood that she wasn't their woman and in no way belonged to them.

Somehow she didn't feel confident that it would go over very well.

Chapter Ten

Hawk wanted to growl at the woman. She defied all his knowledge of women in general. She didn't like that he'd paid for her meal. She hadn't spent hours shopping and had paid for her own shoes. Any woman he'd ever dated had expected him to foot the bill for everything including their apartments if they weren't living with him. Fuck, most women would throw a fit if he complained that they were spending too much money on something.

Jackie wasn't like that. She was independent to a fault and stubborn as a five-year-old kid demanding ice-cream. It was part of her attraction and a good bit of his frustration over the entire situation.

They'd been ordered by their president to keep her in their sights in case she was a spy for the One-Niners, but that had gotten complicated when he realized that he was a little more than physically attracted to her. Her strength of character and the way she'd fought to live at the end of her ordeal meant something to him. He admired her for it.

Now she was fighting the need he had to take care of her. He and Gunner needed to have a hard talk. Hawk wanted to be sure Gunner was on the same foot when it came to taking care of Jackie. They had shared women in the past, but he wasn't as keen on sharing Jackie. He saw her as more than just a sweet butt or bounce around the house type. He wanted her for more than a few weeks. He wanted her long term. How long term? He wasn't sure yet.

The second the door to the motel room closed behind them, she turned on them and started talking. It amused the hell out of him to see her pointing her finger at them.

"I'm not yours to take care of or watch or what the fuck ever you've got in your heads. I'm not your woman, and you won't boss me around. Got it?"

Gunner walked over to her and looked down into her upturned face. "There's where you're wrong. You're our woman. We've claimed you to the club so that no one else can bother you. That means they go through us to get to you. Got it?"

"What do you mean?"

Hawk took Gunner's lead and went with it. "If you're not off the table here, then you're fair game for anyone. We figured you'd be better off with us as your men than bouncing around trying to fight off the other guys. Not to mention any other biker group that stops by for a drink now and then."

"Are you fucking kidding me? I either have to go along with you two or it's fifty or so other guys I'll have to deal with?" She drew in a deep breath.

The motion jerked Hawk's gaze to her heaving breasts. His mouth watered, but her next comment had him lifting his eyes back to hers.

"Why you two? Why shouldn't I pick out my own men?" she asked.

"Because we've already claimed you, and if you try and go after anyone else, they'll refuse to mess with you. We don't like it when women try and cause fights between club members so once someone's claimed a lady, she's off the table, meaning they can't go after her even if she approaches them until her claimers release her."

"That's barbaric and not all that different from what I've already dealt with. I don't like bullies."

Gunner backed Jackie up until her back hit the wall. Then he caged her in with both hands. Hawk just watched to be sure nothing got out of hand.

"First of all, we aren't anything like that bastard that hurt you. Second of all, there's no difference than if you were dating someone on the outside world. You wouldn't make plays for your guy's best friend. Third of all." Gunner leaned closer. "You're stuck with us as long as you're here and nothing is going to change that.

With that, he pressed his lips against hers, kissing their woman to seal his words. Hawk slipped over to turn her face toward him when Gunner released her lips. He took her mouth with his and nipped at her bottom lip before releasing her chin.

"Any questions, doll?" he asked.

"Stop calling me doll. I'm not a freaking toy."

"You're pretty as one of those china dolls my sister used to have when we were children."

"My name is Jackie. Jack if you like, but I'm not a doll or a babe." She huffed out the last, directing her gaze toward Gunner.

"Might as well get used to it, Jack. We like giving our woman a love handle."

"Are you kidding me? A love handle?"

Hawk loved how sexy she got when she was riled up. Her eyes darkened from a light, doe brown to a deep, rich brown even as her cheeks heated to a soft pink. He wanted to taste all that fire, but she wasn't ready for that. First, she had to get her feet healed up before they'd approach her for more. He was sure she'd fight her attraction to them, but it was there. The heat of that kiss had proved it to him. She couldn't lie to them that she didn't want them. Maybe to herself, but not to them.

* * * *

"Am I supposed to have some sort of love handle for you guys? Like maybe Tinker Bell or snookums. I bet that would go over real well with the guys down at the bar. What do you think?" She wasn't going to let them get away with calling her what they probably called every woman they'd ever been with.

What am I talking about? I'm not going to be with them. I'm making sure they know that. Right? That is what I'm doing.

"Jackie, we'll call you whatever we want to. You want to give us names, fine, but remember that once we get back to our place when the night's over with? We'll extract our revenge for anything you say or do."

"What?" She took a step to the side and walked around them to put some space between them.

"We don't hurt women, Jackie. What we do is make them feel real good. Sometimes that means we drag out their pleasure until they're begging for release." Hawk cocked his head to one side.

"I'm not sleeping with you guys."

"Sleeping has nothing to do with it, babe." Gunner winked at her.

"Sex then. I'm not having sex."

"I wouldn't count on that, doll. You were pretty okay with those kisses we gave you." Hawk deliberately walked over to the foot of the bed and sat.

Gunner took the only chair, leaving Jackie with nowhere to sit other than the bed to get off her feet. She refused to sit next to Hawk. He'd use it somehow to get her to agree to being their woman. It wasn't happening.

"Sit down, Jackie. Your feet have to be hurting even in those shoes. If you're still planning on working tonight, you need to get off of them." Hawk patted the bed next to him.

She gave in but didn't sit next to the man. Instead, she sat up by the head of the bed and faced Gunner. When he stood and walked over to where she sat, Jackie realized she'd made a mistake in giving in.

"Swing your legs up on the bed and relax. Nothing's going to happen. You need to rest, and we want to talk to you." Gunner picked up her legs and swung them around on the bed. Then he sat next to her.

Hawk walked around to the other side of the bed and sat on that side of her. She was essentially caged in despite trying to avoid it.

"We don't force women to have sex with us, Jackie. But, there's nothing to say that we won't seduce you. We're both attracted to you and have you under our protection. You're a sexy woman and paired with your strength and sassy attitude, it's a fucking aphrodisiac to us." Gunner rested against the headboard with one leg off the bed.

"That attitude makes me want to take you over my knee then fuck you senseless, but not without your consent, doll." Hawk reached up and twirled a strand of her hair around his finger.

Jackie had to hold her breath to keep from moaning at that tiny gesture. They were already seducing her with how they sat close without really touching her. Hawk's finger in her hair tickled along her skin. The slight pull had her neck tingling at the slight tug. She wanted them. She could admit that to herself now but wasn't planning on acting on it. They were off-limits. They carried too much danger with them, and she carried too much baggage with her.

"What are you thinking, babe? I can almost read the thoughts as they cross your face." Hawk pulled on her hair to get her to look at him.

"Nothing."

"Little liar," he said.

"I'm trying to figure out what your game is."

Gunner turned her chin with one finger so that she had to look at him next. "There's no game. We've been completely up front with you, Jackie. You belong to us, and we'll eventually seduce you into our bed."

"I can't compete with there being two of you. I get dizzy just trying to talk to you guys. This isn't fair. Two men are just too much." She shook her head.

"Babe, you don't know what you've missed until you've let us fuck you. We'll rock your world, and you'll never want to leave." Gunner leaned in and kissed the side of her neck. "You'll melt in our arms like fine chocolate and purr like a pussycat."

Jackie had the urge to snuggle into Gunner's warm body but resisted. She knew her body was ripe to betray her, so she made an effort to pull away instead. Giving in to them would be a serious error on her part. They had the ability to hurt her emotionally even more so than physically. She was almost positive they weren't a threat to her life, but she was very sure they were one to her psyche.

"I need a nap before I go in to work tonight. I can't do that with you guys here. I have just enough time if you'll leave now."

The two men exchanged looks then seemed to come to a decision. They climbed off the bed and walked over to the door.

"One of us will pick you up at five forty-five to take you to the bar. Don't leave without us," Gunner said.

"You don't need to walk all the way to the bar on those feet." Hawk opened the motel room door. "Understand?"

"Okay. Just don't be late or all bets are off. I'm not going to be late because of you guys."

As the last one through the door, Gunner winked at her before closing it so that the automatic lock clicked. Jackie sighed as the overwhelming thickness in the air while they'd been in the room slowly fell away. She could breathe without feeling her heartbeat in her throat again.

If they really do try to seduce me, I'm toast. I can barely resist their lure when they're just teasing. How will I ever be able to hold off once they put their mind to it?

She knew that she'd have to change her panties before going to work. They were wet from just the little time they had been sitting on the bed next to her. Her skin had been hyperfocused on every move they made and had reacted with ice crystals up and down her spine.

Did she want to resist them?

Hell yes she did.

Why?

Because they could eat her up and spit her out, and she'd never see it coming. Jackie knew they were the type of men who could tease her into giving in, hook her on their nasty ways then drop her like an all used up cigarette and crush her beneath the heels of their boots. She didn't want that. She didn't need that. Her mind was already splintered and in need of healing without walking into another round of psych out.

She got out of the bed and turned the air conditioner up to combat the midafternoon heat burning up the concrete outside and smothering anyone who didn't have an air conditioner to fight against it. The one in the room worked great, so she pulled off her clothes and sank beneath the covers after setting the alarm clock for five. She needed a quick shower before she went in to work. Then she'd need to redress her feet before dressing.

Jackie fell asleep after only a few minutes of tossing. It was no wonder she dreamed of the two men. Gunner and Hawk chased her on their bikes while she ran around the town barefooted. Despite hot concrete and splintered glass and rocks, she managed to stay just a little ahead of them. When they cornered her between two buildings, she knew they had her and wasn't afraid.

"You can run pretty damn fast, doll. Why'd you stop?" Hawk asked her.

"I was getting tired, and I knew I'd need my strength when you caught me."

"You were that sure we'd catch you?" Gunner asked.

"I knew I didn't have a chance with there being two of you. If there'd only been one, I wouldn't have been caught."

"Get on my bike, babe. We need to ride. There's a storm coming." Gunner patted the seat behind him.

"Are you afraid of the storm, Gunner?" she asked.

"Only with you in our lives. You matter, and the storm will ruin you."

"I don't understand."

"Just get on the back of his bike, Jackie. There isn't much time. Hurry, woman. Hurry."

She started walking toward Gunner and his bike but the wind picked up, and she had to lean forward and push hard to make any headway.

"Hurry!"

Jackie cried out, reaching with both arms for Gunner. Somehow she knew that if she didn't make it to his bike, all would be lost.

His hand reached out and clasped hers, but just when she thought the wind would win, Jackie woke to the sound of the alarm clock with a scream on her lips.

Chapter Eleven

Gunner sat next to Hawk at the table as the rest of the group shuffled in. Church, as they called their type of management meeting started at nine sharp this morning. Everyone parked their weapons out front where one of the other club members guarded them. No weapons in the meeting. Tempers tended to flare up, and emotions ran high in some of them. It was safer for everyone that no one had access to guns or knives until it was over.

"Come to order, assholes." Terror banged the gavel on the wood table. "Loco, old business?"

They dealt with the normal issues like minutes, treasurer's report, the report on getting their new businesses going. Despite having the store set up and ready for inventory, no one knew what to order or how to stock the place. They had plenty of stiffs who could work the counter and Bush could handle the books, but they needed someone who knew enough about cars, trucks, bikes, and farm equipment to order the right parts they needed to keep in stock without making the store stock heavy.

There was a fair amount of arguing among the group, but nothing was solved. Gunner thought of something. He remembered Jackie saying she'd fix her own damn truck if she could just get the parts. Maybe she'd know enough to help them out while she was there.

"Got an idea," he called out as Bush and Loco argued over who would make the first order.

"Shut the fuck up, everyone!" Rage nodded toward him. "What's the idea?"

"Jackie said something about doing the work on her truck herself once she got the parts. If she knows enough to fix a busted radiator, she probably knows enough to help set up an initial parts order for the store."

"We don't know if she's trustworthy yet. Why would we trust her with our store?" Terror asked.

"We all look through what she's ordered, and if it looks off, we don't use it. Personally, I think it's our best bet. Won't hurt to ask her some questions and see what she knows before we ask her to set up an order."

"Plus, we can keep a closer eye on her outside of the bar that way," Hawk added.

Terror and Rage exchanged looks. Rage spoke up. "We'll talk to her and see what she feels like. Does everyone agree to let her make the order if we're satisfied with her?"

There were two noes and five yeses.

"Now what have we learned about the One-Niners?" Terror asked.

"There are four in town. Not sure where they are staying since they aren't at the motel and we haven't found a campsite anywhere," Loco said. "Jinx and Cowboy are trying to keep track of them, but they aren't sticking together. They're splitting up, walking the town, riding the highway. My take is that we need to pick the weakest looking link and sweat him."

"It may come down to that, but I'd like to see if they make any move that will let us know what they are planning. Once we tip our hand and take one of their guys, they're going to ramp up whatever plan they have waiting. I'd like to take them by surprise instead of the other way around." Terror leaned back in the chair.

Gunner agreed with Terror. Once they became aware that they were being followed and watched, their plan of surprising them would be gone.

"Snickers, you and Bush take one of the other guys and get Scooby and Bear to fill in as they can. We need more information. Where are they staying, and do they have friends in town?"

"There are several empty houses scattered around. They've probably set up camp in one of them. We can search through them," Hawk suggested.

"Do that, but be very careful. Don't tip our hand. If they know we're onto them, they'll either attack or change tactics, and we'll be back at square one with no one to watch." Terror picked up the gavel. "Any more news?"

No one said anything. He banged the gavel on the table and dismissed them.

"Gunner, bring Jackie over as soon as she gets up. We'll talk to her about the store and see what we think." Rage stood and stretched.

"Will do. How's Mia doing?"

"She's fine. She's enjoying fixing up the house."

"Any pink frilly curtains yet?" he asked.

Rage laughed. "Fuck, no. She knows we won't tolerate pink anything."

"Admit it. If she put pink sheets on the bed, you wouldn't refuse to jump her in it." Hawk laughed. "You guys are so hung up on her you'd let her paint your toenails pink."

"Fuck you, man. Go get Jackie." Rage walked around the huge table and stepped out of the room to pick up his weapons. Hawk and Gunner followed him out and tucked their knives and guns back into their pants and boots.

"Think she's up now?" Hawk grabbed his knives and shoved them back in their sheaths.

"If it's up to me, I'm happy to find out."

"Let's go see."

* * * *

Jackie hoped that the leaders of the MC that Hawk and Gunner belonged to weren't mad at her for some reason. The guys hadn't exactly said anything about why they wanted to see her. Only that they wanted to see her.

"How much do you know about cars and trucks?" Rage asked.

Jackie narrowed her eyes. "What?"

"Gunner and Hawk said you can work on vehicles. I want to know how much."

She looked over at the two men who'd woken her up at almost eleven to drag her over to their clubhouse. What were they up to?

"I know enough to fix my truck if I need to. Why?"

"Would you know enough to help us order parts to open up our parts store?"

"You're opening a parts store here?"

"Yes. Everything is ready, but we need inventory, and all we know are bike parts. We're not as familiar with car and trucks. Plus, there's a big need for tractor and farm equipment parts here, as well." Rage sat back in the chair.

"I used to work in a parts store as well as a garage. I can help with setting up an order. Not as comfortable with farm stuff, but we can always call a farmer and ask what they normally need." She was surprised that they would trust her with something like that.

"Good. We'll set you up at the store to work on the order. No more working as the cook. They still need you to wait tables from nine until close, though," Rage told her.

"Okay. Why didn't you just ask the guy at the garage?"

"Believe it or not, he said he couldn't help us. Said he wasn't up on all the fancy gadgets. Plus, he's wanting to retire." Rage stood, indicating the meeting was over. "Gunner and Hawk will make sure you have whatever you need. We've got several parts magazines and company information for you to use to set all of it up."

"When do I start?" she asked.

"Now. The faster you get the inventory ordered, the sooner we can open."

Jackie looked over at Hawk. "Let's go then."

She followed Hawk out of the office and across the common area of the clubhouse. There were several women cleaning up the place, but none of them even looked her way. She assumed they were the club girls she knew most every MC kept around for fun and games. She wouldn't allow herself to ever become one of them.

But isn't that exactly what I've become? A club woman?

She slammed that door. She wasn't a club whore. She was just under the protection of Hawk and Gunner. That was all. They weren't sleeping together, and she'd fight her hormones every step of the way if it meant remaining independent.

"Climb on, babe." Gunner started the motorcycle and waited for her to strap on the helmet and climb on back of the bike.

Hawk mounted his bike and gunned the engine once he was ready. They took off out of the clubhouse parking lot. She could tell the two men were talking to each other using the mics in the helmets, but hers didn't have a mic for communication. It didn't really bother her. She doubted they would be talking about anything that interested her.

They raced through town to a little building not far from the garage where her truck sat forlornly next to a dumpster. Maybe she would be able to work on her truck sooner with the new job. Surely it would pay more than the cook's position at the bar.

The building had a large plate glass window in front and one glass door. The light red brick looked to have been recently sandblasted. There were plenty of parking places to handle customers and a loading dock to one side at the back. The guys parked next to the front door and cut their engines.

Jackie slid off and waited for the guys to do the same. Hawk reached into his pocket and pulled out a key.

"Wait until I disarm the alarm before you come in," he told her.

She followed Gunner inside once the alarm had been taken care of. There were shelves already in place and ready for merchandise. She hoped she could help them, or she wasn't sure what they'd do to her if she failed to order in the right mix of parts.

I don't plan to be here when they open. As soon as I get the parts for my truck and get it going again, I'm out of here.

That was her plan. She wouldn't stick around to let the two guys talk her into sleeping with them. Sleeping with them would complicate things more than she wanted to deal with.

"Come on back to the office. You can set up in here for now. We've got books for you to use along with a list of the things that the old man says he has to order all the time. We have a list of bike parts we want on hand that you can order while you're ordering everything else." Hawk showed her the list printed out in neat handwriting.

"We're planning to take over Sully's garage to handle his business so he can retire, and bring in new business by adding the custom bike side. We may even branch over into custom car designs. Mostly paint jobs and body modifications." Gunner propped one hip on the desk. "There's a good market for the bikes, so if we tap into anything that looks like cars will be just as profitable, we'll hire in for that line of business."

"So, for right now, I'm ordering the list of bike parts here." She indicated the list on the desk. "The list of parts that the guy at the garage normally orders, and anything I think a parts store should keep on hand."

"That's it." Hawk leaned back against the doorjamb. "Can you handle it?"

"Yeah. I think I can handle it. I need to know a few things. How many people live here and in the surrounding areas that might come in for anything? Also, on the custom bike and the parts list for the shop, do you get long distance orders for the bikes? I'll need to take all of that into consideration to figure the units you need on hand."

Hawk and Gunner exchanged looks.

"Good point." Hawk nodded. "We'll get that information. Can you start on it without the information?"

"Yes. I can do that. Let me ask you a question, though. Say you use a specific spark plug for the majority of the bikes you work on, how many would you think you would use in a week's time?"

"Okay, I see what you're getting at. I can provide you with the list of orders we've made over the past six months. How about that?" Gunner asked.

"Perfect. That will help me figure out how heavy you want to carry certain items. Some will only be one or two each, and some you may want a case of them. I'm awake and ready, so let me get started," Jackie said.

"That's the plan. Look around and let us know if there's anything you need right away." Hawk opened drawers in the desk indicating pens, pencils, paperclips, and such.

Gunner tore out a piece of paper from a scrap pad and printed something on it before handing it over to her.

"Those are our cell phone numbers in case you need us before we come back to pick you up. We'll run by the diner and bring you a hamburger. That sound okay to you?" Hawk asked.

"Fine with me. No mustard on the burger." She smiled, then sat behind the desk and started flipping through the catalogs to get an idea of how they were organized.

She gave the two men an absent wave when they said they were locking the door behind them. She could see that this was going to be a big undertaking. She decided to start with what they wanted for the motorcycle side of the business with the idea that she could add to the numbers once she had access to their purchase orders later.

The bike books weren't the easiest of things to look at. She had to flip through pages more than she thought she would when the name they called something wasn't listed in the index. By the time they returned with her burger, Jackie had the beginnings of a headache behind her eyes. Why did they make catalog print so tiny?

She didn't talk to Hawk or Gunner when they stopped by, just thanked them for the hamburger and Diet Coke as she continued flipping through pages. They disappeared, and the building grew quiet once more except for the normal creaks and groans of an older building.

I sure hope I haven't bitten off more than I can chew. I'm not going to want to do anything by the time they come get me to work tonight.

At least she was off her feet so that her blisters had a chance to heal. She wasn't even sure what time they planned to pick her back up. Was it six or nine? Jackie just shrugged and continued making a list from each catalog. It didn't help that thoughts of the two men continued to race around in her head. When Gunner had perched on the edge of the desk, so that his hip was inches from her face, Jackie had nearly reached out to touch it.

Sheesh, she was worse than a schoolgirl finding herself sitting next to her secret crush. She had to stop thinking about them in that way. She wasn't going to sleep with them. Oh, hell. Now her mind started trying to picture them naked. She groaned and beat her head against the desk, which did nothing good for her headache.

I'm going to cave and let them take me to bed. I just know it.

Chapter Twelve

"Got Jackie set up at the store. She has our phone numbers if she needs one of us." Gunner plopped down in the chair across from where Terror sat behind a desk. Rage had twisted a chair around backward and was sitting on it with both arms folded across the back.

"Is the phone set up so that if she makes a call out, we can listen?" Rage asked.

"Yep. When she picks up, Loco will get a signal and can pick up and listen in without her knowing it." Gunner didn't like that they were treating her like a possible traitor.

She belonged to them. She wasn't a One-Niner. Gunner was sure of it.

I know she's not a part of any plot to get rid of us. I can feel her attraction to us. It's just a matter of time before she's in our bed.

"Think she'll be able to set up our order and get the store stocked within the next month?" Terror asked.

"Yeah. I think so. She needs our purchase orders for the last six months on the bikes to make sure she orders the right number of units. She asked some good questions." Hawk continued standing next to Gunner with his arms crossed.

The phone rang, interrupting their conversation. Terror picked up then jumped up out of his chair, knocking it so that it rolled back and hit the wall behind him.

"What the fuck? Where are you? Are you okay?" Terror's voice had deepened into a low rumble.

"What is it?" Rage had come to stand next to his brother.

"It's Mia. Someone just tried to kidnap her. She sprayed them with mace and was able to get away from them. She's at the diner." Terror shoved the phone at Hawk. "Stay on the phone with her until we get there."

Gunner watched as the two men raced out of the office, heading for their bikes. He didn't blame them for the looks of pure rage they had. He'd feel the same way if anything happened to Jackie.

That stopped him. Wait. What? Jackie's not forever. She's for right now. She had plans of leaving just as soon as she had her truck fixed and roadworthy. Did he really mean that?

Hell. I'm so fucked up. I already have her as my old lady, and there's more than just me to figure into this. Hawk's pretty damn attached to her, as well.

Could they make it work if they could convince her to stay? Could he and Hawk share a woman like Terror and Rage did? He wasn't sure. He wasn't even sure that he cared that deeply for her, but it felt right. She felt right for them.

"They're on their way, Mia. Just stay right where you are. Anyone you don't know walks through that door, hit them with the mace." Hawk continued to talk to Mia over the phone.

A few minutes later, the sounds of Terror and Rage could be heard over the phone. Hawk hung up after talking to Rage for a few seconds.

"Can you believe the bastards tried to take their woman? That's not going to go over well with Rage and Terror. Call Loco and the others to fill them in. We need to meet and figure out what our next step is. I'm sure Rage will stay with Mia while Terror heads up the meeting."

Gunner pulled out his cell and started making phone calls. There was a very good chance they were about to go to war.

* * * *

"It's great to meet you, Mia. I'm Jackie, but everyone up here just calls me Jack." She liked the dark-haired woman Gunner had introduced her to when they'd arrived at the bar.

They'd told her that someone had tried to take her off the street earlier that afternoon. She couldn't imagine how the woman was able to sit still and look so unaffected by it. Of course, she was safe now, between her two men, Terror and Rage the MC's presidents. Still, Jackie was pretty sure she would have still been shaking.

"I'm glad you're okay. That had to be scary as hell." Jackie shouldered the tray with the group's empties.

"It was, but when I sprayed the guys with the mace, they rolled around on the ground screaming like little babies. It's just too bad they were already gone by the time the guys got to the diner."

"Well I doubt you'll be able to do anything without a shadow until they get these guys."

"I know." She smiled but sighed. "They were already overprotective before this happened. Now I'll feel like I'm under house arrest or something."

Jackie chuckled with the other woman then returned to the bar to place her order for the next round of drinks.

The rest of the night flew past. They were busy and the crowd a bit rowdy after the attempt to kidnap Mia. There were more club members there than she'd ever seen before. She recognized a few different insignias of other clubs, as well. She guessed they must be partners or have an agreement with The Howling Death MC in order to drink there.

Club life seemed complicated to her. She knew that Terror and Rage shared being president of the club and that Hawk was the vice president. She wasn't sure what Gunner's position as sergeant at arms represented. She had no intentions of asking any questions. The less she knew, the better for all of them. She had no plans to stick around once she had her truck up and running. She'd make damn sure she checked everything and replaced everything else that was left just to be safe. She couldn't afford for this to happen again.

After work that night, Jackie climbed on back of Hawk's bike more than ready for bed. She was exhausted. Even though she hadn't worked on her feet as long that night, she'd been up and bent over a desk working all day.

When they stopped at the motel, the guys got off with her. She started to tell them that they didn't have to go inside but realized they were in protection mode and planned to be sure she was safe.

"Thanks for the ride back. What time will you pick me up tomorrow?"

Hawk's mouth curved up into a half smile. "We're not picking you up tomorrow."

"What?"

"You're coming home with us tonight. We're just picking up your stuff. We'll move the rest tomorrow." Gunner's smile promised all sorts of wicked things.

She shook her head. "I'm not going home with you guys. I may be under your protection, but I'm not your property or your plaything."

"That's right, you're under our protection, which means you're coming home with us so that nothing happens to you. We can't predict what the One-Niners will do next. It's possible they'll target you if they can't get to Mia. That's not acceptable. You're our responsibility. Now pack what you need for a couple of days, and we'll pick up the rest tomorrow." Hawk picked up her pack from the table and handed it to her.

"You're serious, aren't you." Jackie realized that for the first time, she was worried.

It hadn't occurred to her that she could be in danger by being around the MC members. If the One-Niners thought she meant something to Gunner and Hawk, they might try to abduct her, as well. She sighed and dropped the pack on the bed and began gathering what she'd need. By the time she had the bag packed, she was ready to lie down.

"This is it."

"Good," Hawk said. "Let's get you home so you can sleep. You look dead on your feet, doll."

"Can you stop with the doll, already?"

He chuckled. "How about sweet thing?"

"Whatever."

* * * *

Gunner had enjoyed the feel of Jackie's arms wrapped around his waist, and her lush breasts pressed tightly against his back as he rode through town. His cock had been rock hard by the time they'd made it to their little house.

There'd been a short argument about the sleeping arrangements when they'd gotten her home last night, but she'd been so tired, she'd given in with a warning that they'd better not touch her. Lying there with her sleeping between him and Hawk had been the sweetest of torture. It wouldn't be long until they had her between them as they fucked her.

Needless to say, sleep did things to a person. They'd woken up to find her wrapped around Hawk's body as if she were glued to it. That hadn't left her in a good mood for the morning.

Now she was wrapped around him as they rode to the store that morning. Once again, he was going to be stuck with a boner when they arrived at the store. She'd have no choice but to notice it when they climbed off the bike. His jeans were too constrictive. His dick ached. No doubt she'd try to ignore it.

He nearly laughed at the thought but didn't want to risk Jackie letting go of him for some reason. Her safety was too important. They'd check on her throughout the day while she was at the store ordering inventory.

"What's so funny, man? I can hear you snickering over the mic," Hawk asked.

"Just thinking about how pissed she was this morning when she woke up plastered to you."

"You weren't jealous?"

"Hell yeah, but I can deal with it. It'll be me at some point."

"I can't lie there another night without having her, Gunner. She tastes too sweet."

"I feel the same way, but we've got to go slow and seduce her. She's a fighter, and I guarantee she's already fighting her attraction to us."

"I agree. I've seen her looking at you and lick her lips. Won't be long."

They pulled up outside the store after stopping by the diner to pick up breakfast. The three of them entered once the alarm was disarmed.

"We stocked the fridge with Diet Coke and water for you. Have a seat and eat, babe." Gunner pulled out three waters and set them on the front counter where they could all spread out to eat.

"I put the box of invoices from the bike shop on the desk, Jackie. That should help you figure out what we order. If you have any trouble reading any of it, give one of us a call. We can probably figure it out over the phone. If not, we'll stop by at some point and decipher it for you." Hawk bit into his breakfast sandwich.

Gunner washed a bite down with his water then nodded to the front door. "That stays locked just like the back door. Don't let anyone in but us. Not even another member of the club. Got it?"

"Got it. I don't plan to even go to the doors. You guys have the key anyway."

"The back door will open from the inside if you unlock the deadbolt. It's a safety measure in case of fire."

"We're going to be tied up for about two hours this morning in a meeting. If you call, leave a message. If it's an emergency, call this number and tell them what's wrong." He handed her piece of paper with a number scratched on it. "They'll interrupt and get us."

"I don't plan on needing you guys for anything. If I have questions about any of the invoices, I'll hold them until dinner. Will you be able to bring me something to eat?" she asked.

"Probably be close to five, though. You go in at six tonight to wait tables." Gunner crowded her after finishing his meal. "Burger okay?"

"Yeah. No…"

"Mustard. We got it," he said, the corners of his mouth turning up in a wide grin.

"Remember, don't open the door for anyone," Hawk reminded her as he gathered up their trash.

"Got it. See you guys later." She turned to head to the back to the office, but Gunner stopped her.

"I want my goodbye kiss, babe."

"What?" It was all she got out before his mouth descended on hers.

The kiss held heat as he took it before she relaxed, burning her lips so that she opened to him without hesitation. His tongue swept in and conquered her without so much as a move on her part to stop him. Her body reacted to the demand of the kiss by going soft. Her nipples hardened even as her pussy grew damp with anticipation of more.

He reluctantly released her with one final kiss on her nose and turned her into Hawk's arms.

"Didn't think you'd get away without a kiss, did you?" He laughed. "I've looked forward to this ever since I woke up with you all but on top of me this morning."

"I was asleep. You were warm. That's all there was to it."

He shook his head, a serious expression darkening his face. He took her hand and pressed it against the hard ridge beneath his jeans. He felt huge beneath the denim. She'd felt him when she'd woken up to roll off him, as well. His cock was long and thick, and she wanted him with a fierceness that frightened her.

"This is what you do to me, Jackie. You make me hot and hard. I want to eat that sweet pussy and bury my dick deep inside of you. Get used to it, sweet thing. It's going to happen." He kissed her in a hard, needy way that made her knees shaky. When he released her, she had to hold on to the counter for a few seconds in support.

"We aren't going to have sex."

"Oh, but we are, babe," Gunner told her with his lopsided grin.

"In fact, we'll have sex tonight. Count on it." Hawk nodded at the other man, and the two of them strode to the door and after unlocking it, walked out. She watched Gunner lock the door behind them then speed off on their bikes.

I'm fucked. There's no way I'll be able to resist them if they kiss me like that again.

Jackie was sure that sex with the two of them would be wild and intense, but giving in to them meant a piece of herself would forever be lost. She wasn't a virgin by any stretch of the imagination, but she'd never really enjoyed sex with so much baggage strapped to her back. Would it be any different with them than with any other man she'd been with? Before, there'd always been a relationship of some sort attached to the act. Was there one here?

There can't be. I'm leaving in a few weeks. Just as soon as my truck is running, I'm out of here.

Jackie forced the promise deep down in her head so that she could get to work and pretend that nothing was hanging over her for later that night. She wouldn't think about how just their touch inflamed a need inside her that she'd never felt before.

Chapter Thirteen

"Jackie, you can go on home now. The crowd is winding down, and you've already put in a full day at the store." Scoot took her tray from her.

"I can work my shift. I'm not tired," she argued.

"Appreciate the offer, but Kelly can handle the few guys still left. It's a slow night. Next time I'll let Kelly off. Go on."

She sighed and pulled off the little apron and handed it to him, as well. "Do I go over to the table and let the guys know I'm off, or would that be interrupting anything?"

"You can tell them. They aren't discussing anything secret or they'd be at the clubhouse." Scoot tossed the apron over the bar.

Jackie approached the large table in the back where five of the top club members sat around talking. Terror was there, but Rage wasn't. She had a feeling the other man was with Mia. They weren't leaving her alone at all. The poor woman had been right. House arrest. She shook her head. She was just about in the same boat.

"Hey. I'm off for the night. Want me to sit over there until you guys are ready to go?" she asked.

"You're fine right here. We'll go home in a few minutes." Hawk wrapped an arm around her hips and pulled her down to sit on his lap.

Gunner rested one hand on her thigh and sipped at the beer he held in the other one. Hawk ran his fingertips under her shirt, tickling the skin of her abdomen. She couldn't seem to wiggle to get him to stop, then she felt the evidence of what her scooting around on his lap had created.

Fuck!

The long, hard length of him pressed against her ass. She'd caused that. It hadn't been her intentions, but now she was sure he'd expect her to take care of it. Crap. All his promises rushed forward from the back of her mind to bombard her with images in her head. Her breathing picked up until she was afraid someone would notice it and think that the guys were doing things to her under the table.

Well they are. They're torturing me.

It was a sweet torture but torture nonetheless. She needed to calm her breathing and be still. It wasn't easy with Hawk's boner for company. It kept putting ideas in her head that she was sure had her face turning red by the way her cheeks burned.

"Hawk, I think it's time to go. Poor Jackie is about dead on her feet. She's been up and working for more than twelve hours now." Gunner scooted back from the table and got up.

Hawk nodded and allowed Jackie to slide off his lap with an evil smile as she rubbed her ass along his rock-hard cock. She stood up on wobbly legs and said bye as the guys steered her toward the door.

"Do you know how sexy you look with your face all flushed and that little pink tongue moistening your lips every few minutes?" Gunner cupped her elbow as he leaned in to whisper in her ear once they were outside.

"I—I'm not trying to be."

"That's part of what makes it so hot. It's all natural, not contrived." Hawk kissed her nose then climbed on his bike.

Gunner jerked his head for her to ride with Hawk then climbed on his own bike. They started the big machines up and drove out of the parking lot without stirring up gravel. Probably because of the other men's bikes parked so close to theirs.

Jackie tried to calm her nerves the short trip to their home but had little luck. Their promises hung in the air over her head. She had no doubt they would make good on them. She wanted to refuse them but knew she couldn't. Her body had a mind of its own, and it wanted the two men like a boozer wanted his whiskey.

Once inside the house, she was surprised when the men went about putting away their weapons without so much as a word.

"I'm going to take a shower," Gunner told them then disappeared into the bathroom.

"Can I take one after him?" she asked.

"Sure can, sweet thing. Come here and let me help you out of your clothes." He crooked his finger in her direction.

"I—I can undress myself. Thanks." She backed away from him as she started toeing off her shoes.

"But I want to do it. Don't argue with me, Jackie." He stood and advanced on her. "I'll just win in the end."

She felt like prey before a predator as he backed her into the wall. She had nowhere to go. If she were honest with herself, she didn't really want to be anywhere else except where she was. She didn't have to like it, though.

I'm crazy. I can't want both men. It's just not right. I don't care if Mia can do it. How can I?

"Stretch your arms above your head, Jackie."

She complied without hesitation.

"Leave them there. Don't move unless I tell you to."

She had expected this demand of obedience from Gunner, but not from Hawk. It surprised her into doing exactly what he said. She remained still as he went to his knees and slowly unfastened her jeans. His hands slowly pulled the denim material down over her hips then down her thighs. He held her hand so that she could step out of them when he'd gotten them down to her ankles.

He didn't stand after that. Instead, he used his teeth to pull her panties over her hips and down to her thighs. Then he curled his hands around the waistband and jerked them down, as well.

"Fuck. Your pussy smells so damn good." He breathed in deep then slowly let the air from his lungs.

All Jackie could do was whimper at the dark gaze that caught her as he leaned in. Then he broke eye contact as he held her hips steady so that she could step out of the underwear, as well.

"I'm going to eat this pussy until you beg me to fuck you, Jackie. You're going to come all over my tongue."

"Hawk," she whined. "Please don't say things like that."

"Why? Because it makes you want me as much as I want you?"

She didn't answer him.

"I bet you scream when you come, don't you, sweet thing?"

Again, she couldn't answer him. Her voice felt locked in her throat.

Hawk placed openmouthed kisses all across her pelvis, down her thighs and back up again. He hovered near her mound, inhaling once more before gently biting her belly just below her belly button. Then he groaned.

Jackie moaned with him and shifted on her feet. She wanted what he promised but wasn't about to ask for it. She had a feeling she'd be begging for it before the night was over.

"Shower's free. There won't be enough water for three showers. You better share, guys." He stood in front of them wearing nothing but a towel around his waist.

Jackie struggled to take her eyes off him. His broad chest, damp from the shower, begged for her to lick it. Something inside her stirred, urging her to draw circles around his nipples with her tongue. The look on Gunner's face as he looked her up and down tightened her pussy. The way he lingered on her breasts had her nipples hardening almost painfully. Then what he'd said hit her.

Share a shower with Hawk? That promised to be a disaster.

"No funny business in the shower, though. I don't want one of you to slip and fall."

"Asshole." Hawk, punched him in the arm. "Come on, sweet thing. We'll have to be quick, or the hot water will run out. We need a larger tank."

Jackie allowed Hawk to guide her into the bathroom. The shower tub combination really would make showering together very personal. Hawk turned on the water and adjusted the temperature. When she stepped into the tub, the water felt wonderful against her skin. She always felt nasty and greasy after working at the bar.

"I'll soap you up then you can do the same for me." Hawk lathered up a cloth with soap then rubbed it all over her body, paying extra attention to her breasts. It felt good to have someone wash her back. When he moved lower, she tried to take the cloth from him, but he held it over her head.

"I'm going to wash you all over. Spread your legs, Jackie. The water is going to get cold soon."

Jackie slowly widened her stance, her face burning in embarrassment. How could she do this? Twenty-four hours ago, she'd have laughed at the idea she would be taking a shower with one of the two men. Now look at her. She was spreading her legs to let one of them bathe her down there. She had little doubt they would fuck her tonight. She had no defense against them. She wanted them as much as they wanted her and she wasn't going to fight it.

"There you go. Rinse off, and you can soap me up." His eyes were dark and heavy-lidded. Desire burned there.

Jackie took the cloth from him and began rubbing it over his shoulders and down his arms then across his wide chest. She couldn't stop the brief hesitation in her breathing as she lowered the cloth down the light sprinkling of hair that ran the length of his chest and abdomen to meet up with the hair that crowned the base of his cock.

"Turn around. I want to get your back next."

He complied, and Jackie scrubbed the back of his shoulders and down his back. Then she bit her lip as she washed his ass and down the back of his thighs. His ass was a bitable bit of meat, but she refrained. Instead, she indicated that he should turn around once more, and she was faced with the daunting task of washing his groin.

The massive dick bobbed at her, all hard and engorged. She didn't think the rough cloth would help, so she soaped up her hands, and after a moment's hesitation, Jackie took it in both hands and ran her hands all over the bulbous head and down the hard yet silky shaft then down to the balls. She rolled the sac so that she got every inch of him clean then rinsed out the cloth and handed it back to him.

"You can rinse off now. I'm going to get out to give you room."

"Go on then. I bet Gunner has a towel waiting on you." Hawk stopped her though when she started to step out of the tub. "See you soon."

Jackie was careful when she climbed out of the tub, and sure enough, Gunner stood waiting with a towel outspread for her to walk into. He patted her dry, making sure to get her breasts and pussy.

"Come on, babe. Let's get in the bed where it's cozy and get warmed up." Gunner grinned at her, his mouth turned up in a smile.

"We're going to sleep. I'm not having sex with you." Famous last words if she ever heard them.

"Oh, were going to have sex, babe. Then we'll sleep like babies."

"You'd force me?" she asked, her face burning with anger.

"We don't force women, Jackie. You want us as much as we want you. All it will take is us loving on you, and you'll be more than eager," he said.

"That's seduction."

"Whatever works, babe."

"Seduction is a type of force."

"No, it's foreplay."

Jackie agreed with him, but she didn't have to like it. Why was her body betraying her? She didn't need this kind of complication in her life. She'd be leaving soon. Really, she was going to fix her truck and drive away from the little town and the two men so eager to bed her.

Gunner threw back the covers on the bed and nodded for her to climb in. The second she'd crawled onto the bed, her resolve began to crumble. Her pussy moistened. Her nipples pebbled in anticipation. He climbed on behind her and immediately began kissing her shoulder across her collarbone and up her neck. A soft whimper nearly escaped, but she managed to swallow it down until he nibbled at her jaw. His kiss, when it came, promised all sorts of nasty things. He sucked on her tongue before using his to trace the inside of her mouth. Then he was back to kissing and nipping at her neck and shoulders.

"You started without me. I better catch up." Hawk climbed on the other side of the bed and went directly to her breast, sucking on just her nipple before sucking more of her mound into his mouth. The drawing of his mouth had her pussy contracting, looking for something to squeeze.

Gunner moved down to take her other breast in one hand as his mouth enveloped her nipple to torture her along with Hawk. She found her hands grabbing at their heads, pulling on their hair to keep them there.

"I'm going to eat that pretty pussy of yours, sweet thing. I bet you taste better than candy." Hawk moved down her abdomen, licking and sucking at her skin.

His tongue lapped at the little indentions where her pelvis met her thighs, causing her to buck against the bed.

"God, yes." She wanted him to suck her clit.

"Won't be long before you scream for us, babe." Gunner moved from one breast to the other and back again.

"Please." Her keening cry ended in a whimper.

Hawk crawled between her legs and stretched out with his legs hanging off the bed. He spread her thighs wide and blew lightly across her wet pussy lips. She shivered more in anticipation than at the cool air. Her body burned with need.

He leaned in and drew his tongue up her pussy, then spread her engorged lips and licked up and down her slit until she was squirming on the bed beneath him. When he circled her clit, Jackie tried to follow him by moving her hips to get him to rub across the little nub with his tongue, but he didn't.

"Hawk!"

"Easy, babe. He'll take care of you. Let him build that need until you scream your orgasm." Gunner moved back up her body to draw her mouth in another sensuous kiss.

Her body was on fire. She needed to come something terrible. She thought she'd explode if they didn't do something soon.

Then Hawk touched her clit with the tip of his tongue. She felt him slide two fingers inside her as he placed soft kisses on the tiny nub. As he slowly pumped his fingers in and out of her pussy, he sucked the button into his mouth and tickled it with his tongue. She exploded around him without giving her a chance to breathe. Then when she finally drew in a deep breath, she screamed just like he'd promised she would. The pleasure poured out of her mouth in another wordless cry.

"There's my sweet thing. You taste better than cotton candy." Hawk crawled up her body. "I want that equally sweet mouth around my cock."

Gunner took Hawk's position between her legs as the other man knelt next to her head. Gunner rubbed the rounded head of his cock up and down her slit, spreading her juices all over the tip. He pressed against her until she welcomed him by allowing him entrance. He pumped in and out, gaining a little more with each tiny thrust. When he'd finally made it all the way inside her cunt, bumping softly against her cervix, she breathed out a soft sigh.

"Tight. So fucking tight." Gunner's strained voice added another flair of arousal to her already overwhelmed body.

"Suck my cock, Jackie. Open that sweet mouth and take me inside. I want to feel your throat tighten around me." Hawk fisted his dick at the base and rubbed it over her lips.

Jackie opened to him, taking in just the head and sliding her tongue over the slit, tasting the pre-cum as she did. He tasted salty.

She ran her tongue around beneath the ridge of the cockhead then lathed up and down his stalk before taking as much of him as she could down her throat. He bucked but kept his hand at the base of his dick to be sure he didn't choke her.

"Yeah. Just like that. Swallow around it, babe."

She did. Working her throat over the thickness of him then pulling back to suck on just the head again. She started back down, relaxing her throat to take more of him then swallowed down, making the big man groan as she did.

"Fuuuck." He drew out the word as she swallowed a second time.

Gunner thrust in and out of her in slow, measured pushes that went deep and hard. She could already feel another climax building in her body. Could she go again? She never had before.

Every other time, Gunner rubbed over that sweet spot she'd never noticed before. It felt so damn good. She found herself arching her back into his thrusts. He held her hips in his hands, pulling them as he thrust inside her, then pushed them away as he pulled back out. Jackie was going to climax again. They were ruining her for any other man. Leaving them would be like tearing away a piece of her. How would she ever get up the strength to drive away?

Chapter Fourteen

Dear God, she was so freaking close. They were teasing her, killing her with the pressure building inside her. She'd die when she came. She was sure of it.

Gunner quickened his pace, pounding into her with enough force it scooted her up the bed even as Hawk held his cock so that it moved in and out of her mouth as she sucked the thick dick with all her strength. He groaned each time she swallowed around him. It became a need for her to make him come in her mouth. She wanted to suck him dry.

"Fuck, yeah, babe. Just like that. I am so fucking close."

She doubled her efforts. She wanted him to come before she did. One hand massaged her head then pulled at her hair then back to massaging. She lightly raked her teeth over the long length of him before sucking for all her worth. Hawk roared, cum spurting in her mouth and down her throat. She swallowed convulsively in an attempt to take it all.

"Motherfucker!"

She swallowed until he stopped, then she licked all around the bulbous head to lick him clean

"That good? Wait until you feel her cunt suck you all the way in and squeeze while you fuck her." Gunner lifted her thighs over his arms and began pumping in and out of her to the point she saw stars as her climax bit into her before she realized it was there. Her scream burned her throat.

"Yes!" Gunner's rhythm faltered as she clamped down on his cock.

He jerked, plunging in one last time and filling her with his cum. She felt the hot spurts against her pussy walls as he emptied himself. He collapsed over her body, burying his face between her breasts.

"Get off of her, asshole. You're too heavy." Hawk pushed Gunner to one side.

"I'm dead. I can't breathe after that." Gunner rolled onto his back panting around his words.

"I think Jackie just snored."

"No I didn't. I'm trying to catch my breath. Dear God. I've never climaxed like that before. I won't be able to move for at least a week." Jackie meant it. She was done.

"You don't have to. Go on to sleep, sweet thing. You've had a full day, and we tuckered you out tonight." Hawk pulled her against his body so that she faced Gunner.

"Good night." She yawned and relaxed so that she was on the edge of sleep when Gunner backed against her and pulled one of her arms over his chest where he held it there with one hand.

Jackie was sure she was a goner for them now. She'd have to think about it when she could string more than a few thoughts together in her head. Things had gotten complicated.

* * * *

Jackie sighed and stared at the list she'd completed. She would need to place three different orders from three separate companies. One specialized in motorcycle parts and the other two specialized in automobile and farm equipment respectively. Now all she needed was a way to order and pay for the parts. They all required a twenty percent payment up front before they'd ship the merchandise.

She checked the time and found that it was close to three thirty in the afternoon. The guys would be at the bar across town. She'd call and ask what she was supposed to do about making the order. They could fax it or place the order online, whichever they preferred, but her part was over.

I guess it's back to cooking and waiting tables.

She didn't mind either, though by the end of the night her feet and calves ached from being on them for so long. She stood and stretched before picking up the phone and dialing Gunner's number. He answered on the third ring.

"Hey, babe. What do you need?"

"I'm finished with making up the order. There are three different companies you'll need to work with. They all three require a twenty percent down payment for the order and net within sixty days of delivery. You can fax, e-mail, or call. Whatever you guys want to do."

"Great work, babe. One of us will pick you up in a little while. Hang tight."

"Nowhere to be and all." She shook her head when he chuckled then hung up.

"Ass."

Jackie walked around the building, looking at the shelves in back waiting for inventory to fill them. The front would have some parts and supplies out in the showroom area, but most of the merchandise would be kept in back. She wondered who they would have minding the counter and if they had any experience.

She had liked working at the parts store the few months she'd filled in for a friend. With her knowledge of motors and mechanics, it had been easy. Maybe she would enjoy working here and put off leaving town.

And maybe not. Hanging around with Hawk and Gunner had a downside. She'd still be there when they got tired of her and moved on. It would hurt, and she'd end up leaving town anyway. It was probably better to leave as soon as her truck was running than to stick around and get her heart broken.

The sound of glass breaking jerked her to her feet from the stool she'd been sitting on in the back.

What the hell?

She ran up front to find herself headed off by two gruff-looking men with long shaggy beards and equally unkempt hair. They wore black vests with various patches adorning the front. She hadn't seen them before and wondered if they were from the notorious One-Niners the guys had been talking about.

"What do you want? There's nothing here right now. The store isn't even operational." She took a step back.

"We want you, bitch. They'll give us what we want to keep you alive," one of them said.

"Who are you?"

"Doesn't matter. What matters is that you are our edge to taking over this town." This came from the other man, the one with a slight crook in his nose.

Both had bloodshot eyes with red rims. She guessed that they were the ones who'd tried to get Mia and had gotten Maced for their effort. Go Mia. But it still left her at their mercy if she couldn't get away from them.

Now would be a good time for the guys to show up. I could really use their help.

"Don't make it worse by running, lady. You won't get far." Crooked nose again.

Jackie knew the door to the back was just behind her. If she could run through the back and make it to the office, she could lock the door and push the desk against the door. Maybe by then Gunner or Hawk will get there to help her.

She feigned giving up by dropping her shoulders then whirled when they let down their guard and raced to the back. She made it to the office, but when she tried to slam the door, one of them got his foot in the door, blocking her efforts. She screamed as she pushed, but she was no match for the two bikers as they hit the door with their combined effort. It knocked her across the small room into the opposite wall, causing her to hit the back of her head.

Stars exploded behind her eyes, and she slid down to the floor and hugged her head. It felt as if she'd jarred everything inside including her teeth. Where were the guys?

"Look, bitch. You keep causing us trouble and I'll knock you out and throw you over my shoulder," crooked nose snarled.

Jackie cringed as the pain in her head settled into a steady throb. The other man reached down and snagged her by the arm, pulling her up from the floor so fast she grew nauseated and nearly threw up. It must have shown on her face because the guy released her and jumped back.

"Fuck, grab her, Jug. Don't let her get loose." The one with the crooked nose shoved the other man on the shoulder.

"I don't want her throwing up on me, Rooster."

"Fuck that." Rooster grabbed her by the other arm and pulled her toward the door.

As they walked through, Jackie dug her fingers into the doorjamb with both hands just trying to slow them down. The bastard just jerked her lose and kept going. She grasped everything she could on the way by, turning over a set of shelves that barely missed all of them.

"You crazy bitch!" He wrenched her out of the way, then shook her so that she gagged from the pain of having her brain rattled again.

This time he threw her over his shoulder. "If you throw up on me I'll make you lick it off. Got it, bitch?"

Jackie couldn't say a word. She was too busy trying to keep her lunch down which wasn't easy hanging upside down.

They walked through the broken entrance and Rooster threw her in the front of a truck then jumped in next to her. He nabbed her ponytail and yanked it hard when she tried to scoot across and out the other side. The pain stopped her cold. How was she going to get out of this? The MC wouldn't lift a hand to save her. She wasn't anything to them except a waitress who'd helped them out with the store inventory. They'd chalk it up as good riddance in all likelihood. It wasn't like she was married or something to anyone.

Mia would have been fought over, but Jackie had no illusions of her fate. Once the One-Niners figured out that they weren't going to give in to their demands, they'd kill her. She could only hope that they would do it quick.

I'm on my own, here. It's up to me to get out of this.

She tried to wiggle free of Rooster's hold but couldn't. She tried to get her feet up to kick at Jug as he drove, but Rooster just pulled her so that she was bent over with her face against her knees.

"She almost made me lose control. Keep her still, man."

"Stop moving around, or I'll knock you out." Rooster hit her hard in the side.

She couldn't help groaning, but it was nothing to what she'd endured all those years ago. She could endure anything if there was a chance at getting away from them.

The truck made several turns she couldn't see, and after about fifteen minutes, they turned down a bumpy road then a short, easier drive before the truck stopped. Jug got out of the truck first then Rooster opened the door and dragged her out by her hair. She managed to land on her feet, but barely. Once again, the big man threw her over his shoulder before she could try to pull loose from his grip.

He carried her up some steps then into a house. The room smelled of smoke, garbage, and unwashed bodies. He strode through the front room into the kitchen then opened a door and stepped down. A sick feeling traveled up her spine. They were going down. A basement. She finally screamed and started fighting him, beating his back and yanking at the belt in his jeans in an effort to get him to drop her. She didn't want to go down there. She really, really didn't.

* * * *

"Why don't you pick up Jackie. Scoot said she's off tonight. I'll grab a few steaks, and we can cook at home tonight," Hawk suggested.

"Sounds righteous. We'll have her the rest of the day and night all to ourselves." Gunner's face lit up at the thought.

He couldn't wait to get in that tight little ass. She'd been liquid heat with her mouth around his cock. He bet she'd be even hotter when he got his dick in her ass. She'd resisted at first, but all it had taken to break through her defenses were their kisses. Jackie had turned out to be wild in bed. Now that he'd had her, he wasn't giving her up. They'd figure out a way to convince her to stay with them. There had to be a way.

He backed his bike out from between the others then pulled out of the lot at a leisurely pace. He couldn't wait to get her on the back of his bike so he could feel her wrapped around him. Gunner thought they might take a little detour to open the bike up some so she'd need to hug him even tighter.

It took him about six minutes to get across town to where the parts store was located. The second he climbed off the bike he knew something was wrong. The front glass door was broken. Glass littered the tile inside the building. He raced inside, calling out as he did.

"Jackie! Answer me."

He checked behind the counter, the back where several metal shelves were tipped over, then the office. It was there that he saw the main struggle. The door was off one hinge and against the wall. It was obvious she'd put up a fight, but where was she? Was she hurt? He didn't see any blood thank, God.

He had his phone out and pushed Hawk's number before he even thought about it.

"Hey, what's up?"

"The One-Niners have Jackie."

"What? Fuck! How do you know?"

"They broke in the front door of the store, and she's missing. There's evidence of a struggle in the building. I don't know of anyone else who would have taken her." Gunner pulled at his hair as he paced up and down the hall. "We've got to find her, Hawk."

"We will. When we do, I'm painting their blood on our jackets. Meet you at the clubhouse."

Gunner ended the call and shoved his phone back in his pocket before racing through the empty building to his bike. It only took him three minutes to pull up outside the clubhouse. Hawk pulled in seconds behind him.

"Was there any blood," Hawk asked.

"No, but she put up a fight."

"I'll kill them for this."

The roar of bikes coming down the gravel road told them that the club was coming together. They waited for their presidents to walk over before following them into the building.

"Any news?" Terror asked.

"Nothing other than she fought. No sign of blood, so we hope she's not injured," Hawk told him. "Who's with Mia?"

"I've got Bear with her. It'll take an army to go through him. If I didn't know better, I'd have to kill him for being in love with our woman."

"No one's called you guys?" Gunner asked.

Rage shook his head. "They're waiting to be sure we know that she's missing. They'll call soon. It's almost five."

"More than likely they've been watching to see what sort of schedule we had with moving her around." Rage clapped Gunner on the shoulder. "I'm sorry, guys. I never thought they'd go after Jackie since she isn't officially part of the club."

"I guess they don't know that," Terror said.

"When this is over, and we have her back," Hawk began. "We're making her our old lady."

"Are you sure about that? You've only known her a few days. I can't see that being long enough for something that serious, guys." Terror folded his arms.

"How long did you know Mia before you knew it was right?" Gunner asked shoving his hands on his hips.

"Point taken." Terror sighed.

"What do you think their demands will be?" Hawk asked.

"They'll want us to leave town. They want this territory now that they've been pushed out of their own. I don't get why they think we're so weak, though." Rage sat at the head of the table.

"They figure that since we're trying to set up a sanctuary territory that we're not going to fight. They're dead wrong, though," Hawk said.

"Damn straight," several of the others agreed.

"Have a seat everyone. Let's see what we've got. Loco show us the map you've been working on." Rage nodded at the other man.

"I've marked all of the known empty buildings and houses within a twenty-mile radius. I don't think they're staying any farther out since they are slinking around town spying on us. Plus, they would want to be close enough to get the drop on us if they see an opportunity." Loco pointed at several of the circles with red X's through them. "These have already been cleared by our people. The rest still need to be checked. There's about twenty-eight left."

"That's too fucking many," Hawk said.

"No way we can cover all of those before they hurt Jackie," Gunner added.

"That's why Loco is tracing any calls that come to the clubhouse phone. We might not be able to pinpoint their exact location, but we should be able to narrow the search area down by over half." Rage looked over at Loco.

"I figure they'll use a cell phone so I can tap into the frequency and figure out what cell towers they're bouncing off of. Since we have areas without coverage, it should be fairly easy to tell. There are three towers in the region. Whichever one they ping off of will give us the area to search." Loco had the map divided into three circular areas that intersected each other in one point.

"How accurate is this?" Gunner asked.

"It's as accurate as where the phone is. If they go to a different point to call us, it will send us in the wrong direction. You have to insist that they put Jackie on the phone so they'll be working off the correct tower." Loco pointed out the three towers with a pencil then sat.

"So all we can do now is wait until they call." Terror leaned back in the chair.

"I fucking hate to wait while she's somewhere scared to death. You don't know her history. She's already been in this kind of situation in the past. It could break her," Hawk told them.

Gunner knew his friend was having a hard time by the gruffness in his voice. He was so angry that worry wasn't even hitting yet. He wanted to beat the hell out of something but didn't want to miss out if they called. He paced instead.

"You wear a hole in that carpet, you're paying to replace it," Terror said. "That's not doing you any good. Sit down and try to relax. We've got to remain calm, or they'll get the upper hand on us. Don't make me order you to stay here, Gunner."

"Fuck that! I'm not staying here when we know where she is." Gunner plopped down in the chair next to Hawk.

They sat waiting for what felt like hours. Finally, at five thirty, the clubhouse phone rang. Rage nodded at Loco then picked it up.

"Yeah?"

"Who the fuck is this?" Rage asked.

"We aren't doing shit unless we know she's alive. Put her on the phone."

Gunner leaned in closer to try to hear the other side of the conversation, but couldn't.

"I don't give a fuck. Either I talk to her or there's no way in hell we'll even move an inch."

"Motherfucker. He hung up." Rage slammed the phone down and looked over at Loco. "Do you have anything?"

"If they call back, I have the area they aren't in, and that leaves two areas. Hopefully they'll call back so we'll know where to look. I'm betting he was calling from a different place."

"What if they don't call back at all?" Hawk asked.

"We start searching and wipe the bastards out. I'm wondering now if this is a small faction of the club instead of the entire MC. Whoever I was talking to didn't have the smarts for this kind of operation, so the president is somewhere else." Rage drummed his fingers on the table then slapped his hand down hard enough that the table shook. "Son of a bitches dare enter our territory and fuck with our people. We're going to wipe the ground with them. Lock and load everyone. As soon as we have an idea of where to look, we ride."

Chapter Fifteen

Cool concrete felt good to her fevered flesh. Jackie wasn't sure how long she'd been down in the basement, or even how long she'd been lying on the floor. With the windows boarded up and the light off, she had no sense of time. She'd screamed for as long as her voice had held out, but more than likely, they were somewhere remote or they would have gagged her.

She'd spent the first part of the time she'd been down there feeling her way around for a weapon or a tool she could use to pry the boards off the window. There was nothing, not even a mattress she could sit on. She found that there were two windows and one door. Other than that, the walls were concrete blocks. She could feel the edges cemented together in roughly six inch by fourteen-inch cinder blocks.

She explored the staircase to see if there was any loose wood on it, but there wasn't. She tried kicking against the bottom rail to loosen it enough she could pull it off, but she missed more often than she hit it since she couldn't see. She had to face it. She was stuck down there until someone came for her.

Jackie weighed her options. She could curl up in the corner under the staircase, or she could wait for someone at the top of the stairs and try to rush them, take them by surprise. Neither option sounded the least bit appealing, but Jackie needed some sort of plan, or she'd go crazy in the dark. It reminded her too much of her former life.

In the end, she decided to wait under the stairs. She'd wait until they turned on the light and started down, then attempt to trip them by reaching through the open stairs. It was the best plan she could come up with without a weapon. She wondered if they'd ever come back down.

Her stomach churned in a combination of hunger and worry. Once they realized that no one would care if something happened to her, she was sure they'd kill her. Or worse. There were always worse things than death. She knew that firsthand.

Deafening silence filled the dark room. Were they even upstairs or had they left, leaving her all alone in the basement never to return at all. She could die of thirst and hunger. The idea of how long it might take sent a line of ants down her spine even as she shivered in fear. She'd been hungry enough to eat a roach before. Thank God there were none down there with her. Or at least she hadn't heard anything scurrying around.

I'm probably going to die down here. They won't let me go even if by some crazy miracle, The Howling Death MC caved to their demands. They have no reason to let me live.

She slid down the back wall beneath the stairs to wait for someone to come. She had no guarantee they would, and she didn't know if tripping someone descending the stairs would even work. At worst, it could mean punishment if he didn't fall. At best, she'd get free from the basement and end up surrounded by more of the crazy bikers.

She settled down to wait and tried to stop the worst-case scenario thoughts from flooding her mind. She'd endured hell. She could endure this.

Noise overhead startled her back into focus. How long had she been drifting? She couldn't tell. She listened, trying to determine how many there were, but the sound was too distorted. Then the sounds moved over to where the door leading down to the basement was. The noise of the lock being thrown then the door opened, and a light was switched on. It blinded her long enough that the man made it down the stairs before she could react and trip him. She cursed and blinked rapidly, trying to get her eyes used to the light.

"Come over here, bitch." The voice was one of the guys who'd taken her.

She shook her head no. He'd have to come for her. She'd fight him tooth and nail.

"Don't make me come get you. I'll make you sorry."

"Screw you and the bike you rode in on." It was the best insult she could come up with in her state of mind.

He chuckled. "Might just be on the menu later, bitch. Now come over here."

"No."

He cursed and stalked over to where she stood in the corner with the stairs over her head. He'd have to bend over to get to her. She'd use that. When he bent, reaching out for her, Jackie jerked his arm and pulled with all her might, making him hit his head then fall forward. She slipped past him and ran for the stairs. She managed to get to the top of the stairs before another man caught her racing across the kitchen. He slammed her up against a wall.

"What the fuck?" He held her there with one hand around her throat. "Jug! Are you okay? How in the hell did she get away?"

"She was under the stairs and made me hit my head when I went to grab her. I'm going to kill that bitch." The man in question emerged from the basement rubbing his head. "Give her to me."

"Settle down. She's got to be able to talk on the phone. Then you can knock her around a little. Make the call."

Jug cursed then pulled out his phone and pressed a few buttons before he held it to his ear.

"Are you ready to do as we say? I've got the bitch for you to talk to."

He listened then smiled. "She's fine, for now."

A few seconds more of listening. "Here she can talk for a second."

The phone was pressed to Jackie's face. "Talk to them."

"Hello?"

"That you, babe?" Gunner's voice reached her, sending hope to her galloping heart.

"Gunner. Are you coming for me? They have me in a basement."

"Bitch! Shut the fuck up." Rooster pulled her by her throat away from the phone then slapped her. "That's all they're getting."

"Guess you heard that. Now, twenty-four hours and we start sending parts if you're not gone." Jug pressed End on the phone and pocketed it. "Better hope they leave. If they don't, I'm going to cut off a finger and wrap it up in a bow for them."

Rooster jerked her from the wall then grabbed one arm and pressed it up behind her back. "It's back down for you."

"Can I have something to drink?" Her voice remained hoarse from all of the screaming she'd done earlier.

"Jug. Get a couple of bottled waters for her. She can ration them out while we're gone."

"Why give her anything. If she dies, we can still cut off her fingers to send to them."

"If they don't bleed they'll know she's dead. Dead people don't bleed, man." Rooster shoved her ahead of him toward the basement door.

Jackie fought him, kicking back and then snagging the doorjamb in an effort to stop him from throwing her down there again. He did just that. Rooster shoved her down the steps so that she ended up tumbling down the last three or four stairs before Jug threw two bottled waters at her. One hit her in the chest while the other one sailed over her head.

"Be careful with them. We're going to be gone for a while." Rooster slammed the door shut, and the click of the lock told her she wouldn't be getting free that way.

* * * *

"He hit her. I heard him." Gunner turned and planted his fist in the wall next to him.

"Calm down." Rage turned to where Loco sat fiddling with his computer. "Do you have their location?"

"I've narrowed it down to this section." The man jumped up out of his chair and pointed to a circular area on the far side of town. "She's somewhere in one of these houses. I'm trying to get plans for them so I can tell you which ones have a basement and which don't. I'll relay them to you over the phone. You can get started clearing them in the meantime."

"Okay. We go in groups of three. If we spot bikes, we call in help."

Rage divided them up so that Snickers went with Hawk and him. Loco made copies of the map, and each group took three houses to search. The three of them raced from the clubhouse and jumped on their bikes to roar toward the first house.

They stopped a quarter mile from the first house and crept on foot so as not to alert them if they were in the house. When they arrived at the house, there were no bikes, but they searched the place anyway, breaking the lock when they couldn't get in. It didn't seem to have a basement or cellar, but that didn't stop them from going through every room and closet in the house. Nothing.

They ran back to the bikes and headed for the second house on their list. This one had three bikes outside it. There was evidence that there had been more from the churned-up gravel leading up to the house.

"Call in the others," Hawk told Snickers. "We're going to look around to see where the other entrances are."

"Be careful and don't go in alone," Snickers warned them.

Gunner followed Hawk as they made a wide circle around the house and mapped out the back door, the door under the carport, and the one leading into the front. They also noticed boarded-up windows at ground level. There was a basement, and with the windows being boarded from the inside, Gunner was sure their Jackie was down there.

"I don't want to wait for backup, Hawk. She's down there now. We don't know what they may be doing to her." Gunner opened and closed his hands into fists over and over.

"We wait. Can't do her any good if we're hurt and can't get to her. We've got plenty of time."

Gunner didn't like it, but Hawk was right. They returned to where Snickers crouched behind some bushes.

"Did you get them?" Hawk asked.

"Yeah. They're all on their way. We're supposed to wait for them." He looked from Hawk to Gunner. "We are waiting, right?"

"There's at least five of them. We don't want to risk one of them getting to Jackie and either killing her or using her as a shield."

"Good choice."

They watched the house, waiting for the others to arrive. It felt like hours to Gunner, but in reality, it was only about thirty minutes before the majority of the club arrived. They'd parked their bikes down the road like Gunner, Hawk, and Snickers had.

"Any movement?" Rage asked.

"No. Not a peep out of them. I'd bet all of them are inside there waiting for us to move out. They'll send a couple to check to see if we're gone closer to time," Hawk said.

"They have to know that we won't leave for any reason," Gunner added.

"I'm sure they probably do. There are only five of them. It's the most any of us have seen since we've been watching them," Jinx told them.

Gunner didn't want to wait any longer. He wanted Jackie out of that basement. "What's the plan?"

"It's nearly full dark. We'll bust in at nine sharp. They'll be taken off guard. How many doors are there?" Rage asked.

"Three. One up front, the carport door, and a sliding glass door around back."

"Okay, everyone at exactly five after seven now?" They all checked their watches. "Snickers, Bush, take the sliding glass door. Jinx and Cowboy, take the front door. Gunner, you and Hawk take the carport door. Rage and I'll go in behind you and hold them down while you find Jackie and get her out of there." Terror looked at all of them. "Straight up nine. Not a second sooner, guys."

They all took their positions around the house with Gunner, Hawk, Rage, and Terror off to the side of the carport behind a five-foot-long row of hedges. They had nearly two hours to wait. Gunner wasn't good at waiting. Never had been. With Jackie down in a basement, he was having even more trouble waiting out the time.

"Easy, man. We'll get her back. She'll be fine once we have her in our arms. Just remember that. If we jump the gun, we risk her safety. Got it?" Hawk was always his voice of reason, but it wasn't helping as much today as it normally did.

"We're going to make a lesson of them and send them packing, guys. I don't want anyone killed. That will bring in the police, and we don't want any trouble. Got it?" Terror's voice held a bite of anger.

Gunner wasn't sure if he could restrain himself. He wanted their balls for what they'd done. He and Rage should want the same thing for nearly kidnapping their woman.

"I know you want blood. You can beat the crap out of them, but we don't kill them. We aren't killing anyone unless they kill one of ours. Then all bets are off," Rage told them.

"Fine." Gunner forced himself to open his fists and relax them against his thighs. "But if she's hurt, you better hold me back."

"Hawk, can you handle him?"

"I might not want to handle him if they've laid a hand on her."

"Fuck, guys. This is serious. We're trying to keep a good reputation with the town here. Killing someone won't go over well." Terror grabbed Gunner's arm and forced him around to look at him.

"I'll help you beat the hell out of them. They touched our woman, but killing them isn't the answer. That will just bring more of them down here for revenge, and the fight won't stop there. You know it won't, Gunner. We all agreed we wanted peace now."

"I know. You're probably right, but she means too much to me to promise I'll keep my head. All I can say is that I'll try."

"Shit. You do that. Hawk, you both need to rein it in, so we don't screw up what we've accomplished so far." Terror shook his head.

Chapter Sixteen

Jackie dozed off at some point. She woke to the sounds of broken glass and scuffling above her. Muffled shouts and yells followed by heavy bumps and what sounded like furniture breaking. Were the guys fighting for some reason? Had The Howling Death MC actually come for her? She didn't know what to expect if the door opened and someone started down the stairs.

She felt her way down the wall until she was opposite the stairs. The noise continued then the cellar door was opened hard enough that it slammed against the opposite wall.

"Jackie!" The sound of Gunner's voice had relief flowing through her like a welcome drink of ice-cold water on a scorching hot day.

"Gunner!" She raced for the stairs as Gunner, followed by Hawk hurried down the steps.

Gunner caught her up in his arms and squeezed her tight enough to break bones before he let her go so that Hawk could do the same. She'd never been so happy to see anyone in her life. Tears leaked from her eyes despite her trying to keep them from falling.

"Are you okay, babe? Did they hurt you?"

"I'm fine now that you're here. I was afraid you wouldn't."

"What the hell? Of course, we were coming for you. You belong to us." Gunner kissed her before Hawk got his chance.

"There's blood on you. Are you two okay?" she asked.

"It's not our blood, babe. We promised we'd draw their blood for what they did. The guys are mopping up right now. Let's get you out of here." Hawk put one hand around her shoulders. Gunner followed them upstairs.

What greeted her in the kitchen was a blood bath. There was evidence that at least two or three of the five men had broken noses. All of them were bleeding profusely from various wounds all over their bodies. There were five of them sitting against the side of one wall, moaning and groaning. A pile of weapons was sitting between Terror and Rage. The six men had a few bruises and cuts that she could see, but none of them looked nearly as beat as the men sitting on the floor in front of them.

"What are you going to do with them?" Jackie asked as her two men urged her out the side door.

"Send them packing with a message to their president that we don't tolerate violence in our town but that if pushed we will push back." Hawk hugged her. "Let's go home."

That sounded good to her. She was ready.

The three of them walked to where the bikes were parked, and Hawk helped her up on the back of Gunner's bike before they took off for the house. She couldn't wait to put the day behind her. She couldn't believe that it had only been five hours since they'd taken her. She felt as if days had passed.

As soon as they made it in the house, the men were all over her. They stripped her then gently bathed her in the tub before taking her to bed. Gunner spread her thighs with an almost desperate need in his eyes. The first touch of his tongue had her crying out in pleasure. She needed this. She needed them to take her and make her theirs. If they didn't want her, she'd die inside. She sure as hell wanted them to want her.

"Babe, you taste so damn good. I was afraid I'd lose you." Gunner returned to eating her pussy with a vengeance.

"God, Gunner. Please."

She could only beg for him to help her reach that point. She wanted to come so badly.

"Not yet, sweet thing. You're coming with us this time. Both of us." Hawk kissed her, exploring her mouth then moving down to lick and bite at her jaw, neck, and earlobe. He sucked at the junction of her neck and shoulder, then nipped at it.

"I want you both. Take me. Make me yours. I don't want to lose you." Jackie couldn't believe she'd allowed the words out.

"You already are ours." Gunner moved up her body and sucked at her nipple before fitting his cock at her opening. "I'm going to fuck you deep and hard, babe."

He pushed his way inside her. She was wet and ready for him, but he was thick and had to wiggle to get in her. She finally relaxed enough that he surged forward with a deep growl.

"Damn, babe. You're so fucking tight I won't last long." He retreated and thrust again and again. Finally, he rolled her over so that she straddled him. He bucked up as she rose and fell with him.

"Hold her down while I get her ready, Gunner." Hawk knelt behind her.

"What are you doing?" she asked.

"We're making you ours. We want to come inside of you at the same time, so Hawk's going to take that pretty little ass while I fuck your warm, wet pussy." Gunner reached up and kissed her between the breasts. Then he was pulling her flat against his chest.

"Easy, sweet thing. I'm not going to hurt you if you relax. Hurting you is the last thing I ever want to do."

Hawk rubbed something cold and wet on her asshole. He pressed his finger inward then pulled it back out. She wasn't alarmed but knew that no matter how much he prepared her, it would sting. She didn't care. She wanted them both and wanted to be theirs forever.

He added more of the cool lubricant and pressed in and out of her back hole several times before adding even more and adding a second finger. It burned, but not too badly. He fucked her with his fingers then forced more of the lube inside her. The next thing she felt was his cockhead pressing against her ass. She tried to relax her muscles, letting Gunner's hands soothe her as he rubbed small circles against her back.

Hawk pressed harder, stretching her even as she tried to push out. When he finally popped through the resistant ring of her ass, she gasped and dropped her head to Gunner's chest.

"There we go. Easy, Jackie. Just let us do all the work." Hawk pushed all the way in with a soft curse while Gunner pulled nearly all the way out of her pussy. Then they switched directions, and she felt like a piece of cheese between two slices of hot bread.

They seesawed in and out of her until the pressure building was so close to exploding she couldn't help but strain toward it. Her ass burned, but a strange sort of pleasure was escalating from it, as well. She'd never known there were pleasure nerves in her ass before now. The guys sweated above and below her. Hawk grasped one hip with his hand and held on to the back of her neck with the other hand.

"Fuck but your ass is so goddamn tight, babe. Fuck but I'm not going to last."

"Neither am I. She's hot and wet and tight, and with you in her ass, it's like forcing my dick through silly putty. I swear she's going to strangle me." Gunner cupped her breasts in his hands, flicking his thumbs over her nipples.

"Please, please not yet. I need to come so badly it hurts."

"We've got you, sweet thing. We're going to take good care of you from now on." Hawk used both hands to hold her hips as he tunneled in and out of her ass.

She could feel the heat from Hawk's body against her back. The burning sensation in her ass had given way to a strange pleasure that helped fuel her need to climax. She needed them to hurry and push her over. She didn't want to be left hanging. Now with as good as she was sure it was going to be.

"I've got you, babe. Just relax." Gunner put one hand between them where he moved his fingers until his thumb found her clit.

"Yes," she hissed as he thumbed it, teasing it then pinching it between this thumb and finger.

Jackie erupted in pleasure, screaming in a high-pitched whine that even she didn't recognize. The two men lost their rhythm and shouted out as they came, filling her body with their semen. The pleasure went on and on as they continued to fuck her until they lost their strength and collapsed beneath and behind her.

"Holy, shit. That was amazing," Hawk grunted.

"Get the fuck off of us, asshole." Gunner's guttural voice proved he was exhausted.

Jackie couldn't make a sound. She was still trying to relearn how to breathe. They'd pounded her into oblivion. She just lay there when Hawk slowly pulled from her ass and collapsed to one side of them.

"You okay, babe?" Gunner asked.

"Not." Breath. "Sure." It was the best she could do.

Hawk chuckled. "Good answer. Me either."

They lay like that for a long time. She wasn't sure if she slept some or not, but Gunner's dick had finally slipped from her, and she felt the sticky residue from her pussy coating her thighs. At the moment, she didn't care. She was too relaxed to move.

"I love you, Jackie." It came from Gunner. She'd thought him asleep.

"I love you, too, sweet thing." Hawk ran his hand up and down her back. "We want you to be our old lady and stay here with us."

"Really? Like marriage?" she asked.

"We can get married if you want to. Being our old lady is the same thing as marriage to us. We want you with us forever." Gunner kissed her softly on the lips.

"I want that, too. I love you both. I didn't think I could after everything, but I do. I love you so damn much it hurts."

"Are you okay to be caught between us?"

"Always."

THE END

WWW.MARLAMONROE.COM

Siren Publishing, Inc.
www.SirenPublishing.com

Lightning Source UK Ltd.
Milton Keynes UK
UKHW02f1352160318
319572UK00006B/920/P